THE TREE THAT OWNS ITSELF

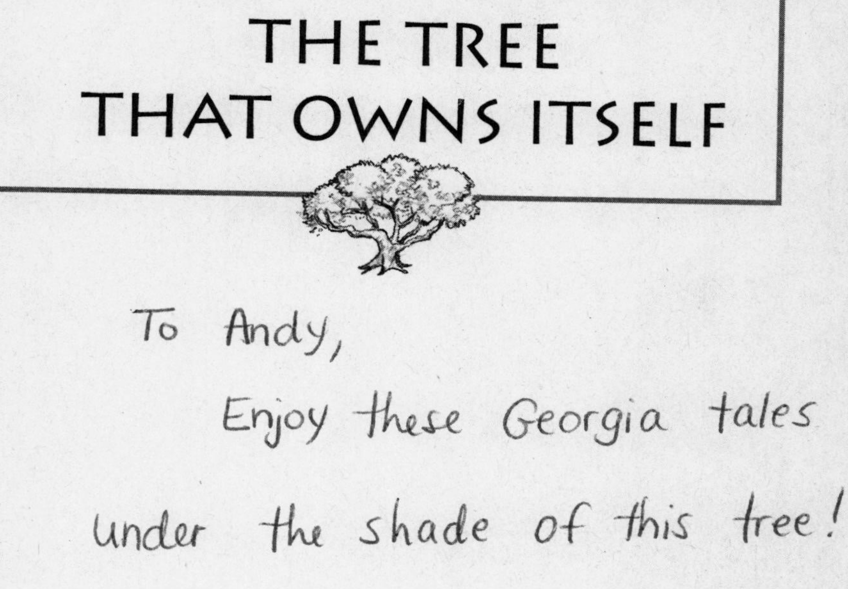

To Andy,

Enjoy these Georgia tales under the shade of this tree!

Gail Karwoski

THE TREE THAT OWNS ITSELF

and Other Adventure Tales from Georgia's Past

LORETTA JOHNSON HAMMER
AND
GAIL LANGER KARWOSKI

ILLUSTRATED BY
JAMES WATLING

PEACHTREE
ATLANTA

JR

A Peachtree Junior Publication

Peachtree Publishers, Ltd.
494 Armour Circle NE
Atlanta, Georgia 30324

Jacket and book design by Loraine M. Balcsik
Composition by Dana Celentano

Manufactured in the United States of America

10 9 8 7 6 5 4 3 2

Library of Congress Cataloguing-in-Publication Data

Hammer, Loretta Johnson
The tree that owns itself and other adventure tales from georgia's past / Loretta Johnson Hammer and Gail Langer Karwoski; illustrated by James Watling.
p. cm.
Summary: Twelve fictional stories from different periods of Georgia history relate the adventures of gypsies, swampers, Cherokees, an Olympic weight lifter, and a parachuting dog.
ISBN 1-56145-120-7
1. Georgia—History—Juvenile fiction. 2. Children's stories, American. [1. Georgia—History—Fiction. 2. Short stories.]
I. Karwoski, Gail, 1949- . II. Watling, James, ill. III. Title.
PZ7.H18424Tr 1996
[Fic]—dc20

95-49365
CIP
AC

To all of Georgia's children,
especially Greg and Stephen Hammer,
Leslie and Geneva Karwoski,
and dozens of kids in our Oconee County classes
who share our love for a tale well told.

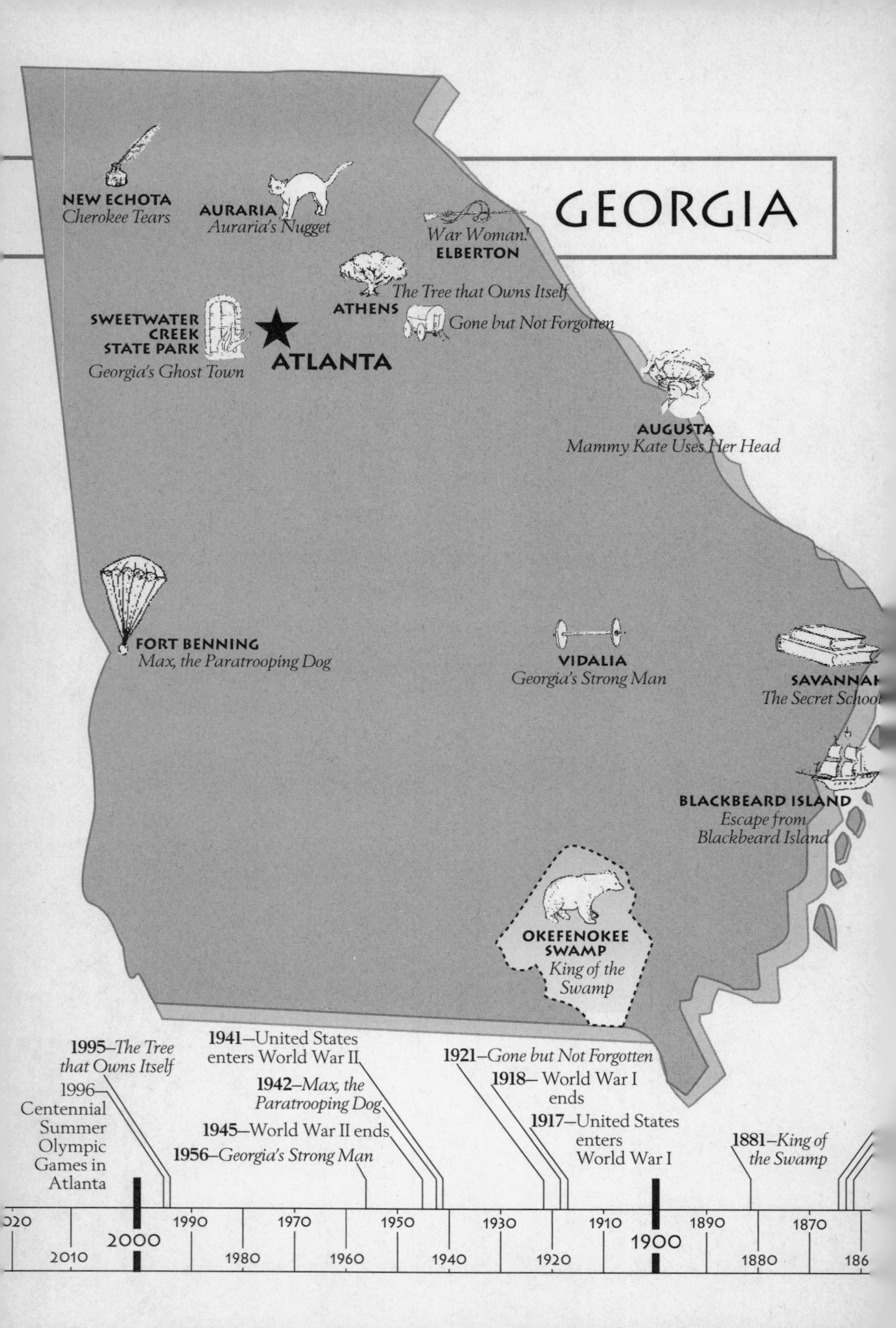
GEORGIA
NEW ECHOTA
Cherokee Tears
AURARIA
Auraria's Nugget
War Woman!
ELBERTON
The Tree that Owns Itself
ATHENS
Gone but Not Forgotten
SWEETWATER CREEK STATE PARK
Georgia's Ghost Town
ATLANTA
AUGUSTA
Mammy Kate Uses Her Head
FORT BENNING
Max, the Paratrooping Dog
VIDALIA
Georgia's Strong Man
The Secret School
BLACKBEARD ISLAND
Escape from Blackbeard Island
OKEFENOKEE SWAMP
King of the Swamp
1995–The Tree that Owns Itself
1996–Centennial Summer Olympic Games in Atlanta
1941–United States enters World War II
1942–Max, the Paratrooping Dog
1945–World War II ends
1956–Georgia's Strong Man
1921–Gone but Not Forgotten
1918– World War I ends
1917–United States enters World War I
1881–King of the Swamp
1990
1970
1950
1930
1910
1890
1870
2000
1900
2010
1980
1960
1940
1920
1880

CONTENTS

TIME LINE

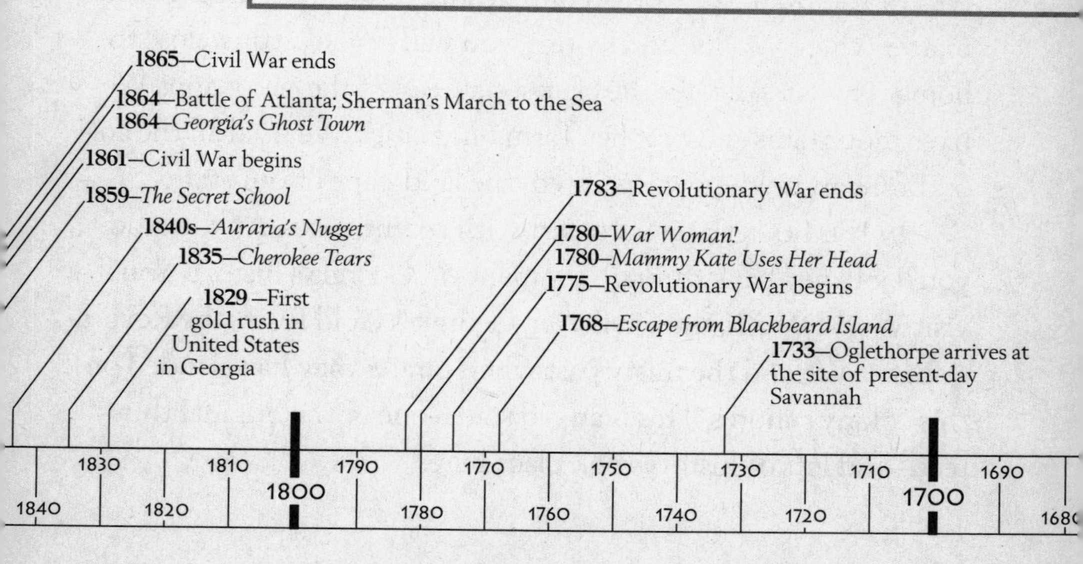

A WARNING FROM THE AUTHORS

DON'T READ THIS NOTE
(Unless you want to know some cool things about this book...)

IN THIS BOOK the stories are about all kinds of folks. You'll meet characters of many shapes and colors: gypsies and soldiers, swampers and Cherokees, an Olympic weight lifter, even a parachuting dog. Prepare to be surprised...these aren't the dull dead people you usually find in textbooks!

IN THIS BOOK the stories are historical fiction, which means that each story is part history and part fiction. But every story is true to the spirit of the time in which it is set; we only played with the facts to keep the stories interesting and moving along. After every story, you will find a note to help you decide how much of what you read is true and how much is made up.

IN THIS BOOK the stories come from every part of Georgia. No matter where you live in Georgia, you will find a setting close to home. This is a BIG state—the biggest state east of the Mississippi. We have mountains and beaches, farms and cities. We used all the colors of Georgia when we "painted" the landscape of our state.

IN THIS BOOK the stories start with recent times. As you read, you'll journey back through moments in Georgia's history. You'll visit World War II, the Civil War, Georgia's Gold Rush, the Revolutionary War, and the misty past when pirates may have landed on this colony's shores. This is an old state—one of the original thirteen—and lots of history took place here.

THE TREE THAT OWNS ITSELF

Famous Places of Athens, Georgia
Journal by Jason Jackson

Monday

Today we began our heritage study. That's what my teacher, Mrs. Miles, calls it. Each kid in the class has to do research on one famous place in our city. We live in Athens, where the University of Georgia is. So there are lots of famous places here.

Mrs. Miles wrote a list of places on the board. She listed the double-barreled cannon at the courthouse, the Lucy Cobb House on Milledge Avenue, the State Botanical Gardens, and a bunch more. Then each of us picked one place. I picked the tree that owns itself. Mrs. Miles says it's on the corner of Finley and Dearing Streets, near downtown. I think it's cool that a tree can own itself.

Now we have to do research to find out about our place. Then we're going to report to the class. Mrs. Miles says we can't just look in one book and copy what it says. We have to use different sources.

We have to keep a record of our work in our journals. We get extra points for having lots of entries. We also get extra points for putting details into our writing. I haven't been doing so great in Mrs. Miles's class so I'm planning to fatten my grade with lots of journal entries. Long, juicy entries—like this one!

Monday night

When I got home from school, I told my mom about my project. She had errands to do downtown, so she said she'd show me the tree.

We went to the Varsity and I got a naked dog, walking. That's Varsity-speak for a plain hot dog to go. We took our food with us and ate under the tree.

Mrs. Miles was right when she said the tree was on the corner of Finley and Dearing Streets! It sits almost in the middle of Finley Street at the corner. Cars can only go in one direction beside it. I'm sure that tree would have been cut down a long time ago if it didn't own its land.

Finley Street is paved in cobblestones, like the streets of long ago. When you go uphill from Broad Street on these smooth, rounded stones, your car goes bumpity-thump. You'd probably have to get your car realigned once a month if all streets were made of cobblestones.

It's a nice tree. It shades the whole circle of land where we sat. My mom says it's a white oak. I don't mean to seem disappointed or anything, but I guess I'm just not a tree freak. I mean, it doesn't look like anything special. It *is* big. It has bark and leaves. I guess it's healthy. But it's just a tree. I know—the tree probably thought I was nothing special, either. Just a boy. Skin. Hair. Really hungry.

But I picked this famous place for my research. And this is the second journal entry I've written on it. So I'm not going to change my topic now.

Tuesday

Our class is in the library doing research. I can't find anything much about the tree that owns itself except this book with a picture of some people planting a tiny tree. You can tell it's a ceremony because they're wearing dresses and suits. The description says they're planting a sapling grown from an acorn of the tree that owns itself. See, the original tree died. So the tree that I saw yesterday was the son (or daughter) of the tree that owns itself. The book also says the tree is a white oak. But my mom already told me that.

Mrs. Miles sent me to the office with a note. She told the secretary to help me dial the Athens Chamber of Commerce. Mrs. Miles said they probably had some information on the tree. The lady at the chamber of commerce was really nice. She said she'd send some information.

Now I'm out of stuff to do. We're in the library for a double period. So Mrs. Miles says I should write down my impressions of the tree. I told her I already did that. But she said I should describe the fence around it. And the sign. I'm really trying to get a good grade on this project. So here goes.

The tree sits up high, in a rounded base of cement or something. It's planted in dirt, and there's some grass and weeds around it. Around the whole circle, there's a fence made of marble posts joined together by a thick chain. There are two marble markers near the tree. One is hard to read, but I think it has the same words as the other one. I wrote down what the marker said yesterday. But I didn't put it in my journal. I was afraid Mrs. Miles would take off points if I copied something. Today, she told me I should use the words. I just have to put quotation marks around them.

This is what the marker says:

"For and in consideration of the great love I bear this tree and the great desire I have for its protection for all time I convey entire possession of itself and all land within eight feet of the tree on all sides. William H. Jackson."

I think it's neat that this guy loved this tree so much. Sort of "The Romance of the Tree." I wonder if the guy had a wife or kids.

I asked the school librarian if Athens has the only tree that owns itself. She looked in some books but couldn't find the answer. So she called the reference desk of the Athens Regional Library. She says they look up information as a free public service. But they were busy. They said they'd call back with the answer. The librarian said she'd write down the answer and give it to me tomorrow.

Wednesday

The librarian sent a slip of paper to me in homeroom. It says:

"The Athens tree that owns itself is not the only such tree. The original tree died and fell in 1942. It was replaced by a sapling from the original. There are other trees that own themselves in other places. But the Athens tree was the first. It is very famous, and other places have copied the idea. It was even written up in *Ripley's Believe It Or Not.*"

Wednesday night

We got the information from the Athens Chamber of Commerce in the mail. It's a sheet of paper describing the tree. It tells the words on the marker. It also tells about Colonel William H. Jackson, who was a professor at the University of Georgia.

The story is that Jackson owned the house and land where the tree stands. He really liked sitting in the shade of this tree. When he got old, he decided to put the tree in his will. He deeded the tree to itself and gave the deed to the city. That's where the words on the marker come from.

The fence came later. A guy named George Foster Peabody saw the tree. He really liked the idea of a tree that owns itself, so he had a fancy fence of marble and chains built around it. Peabody was famous. There's a Peabody Award named for him.

The original tree blew down in a windstorm in 1942. The Junior Ladies' Garden Club decided to plant a sapling in its place. They didn't get the sapling planted until 1946. So there must have been a vacant spot for four years. Maybe Athens had the first dirt that owns itself during those years!

My mom says she'll take me to the Athens Regional Library tomorrow. They have a special room for history research there. It's called the Heritage Room. She said I might find some newspaper articles about the tree.

Thursday

I told Mrs. Miles that my mom is taking me to the library tonight. She announced it to the whole class. She made me tell the students about this special Heritage Room. Then she made me tell about calling the Chamber of Commerce. She said it's important to use many sources when you do research.

I felt like a nerd when I had to brag about my project. But some of the kids said they were going to get their moms to go to the downtown library, too. I think Mrs. Miles really likes my project. Here's hoping for one great big A plus!

Thursday night

I learned a lot about the tree that owns itself at the Heritage Room. For instance:

1. There is no deed for the tree.
2. There is no record that William Jackson left the tree its land in his will.
3. William Jackson never owned any land in Athens. (He did live on the land around the tree for a few years but he was renting the property.)
4. Mr. Jackson was in Macon, not Athens, when he died.

The tree really exists. (I saw it with my own eyes.) But the story about it is a lie. Or a fairy tale.

This is just great. Our projects are due Monday, and the tree that owns itself is a big fake. I'm so mad at the Chamber of Commerce. How come they didn't tell me this is just a made-up story?

Friday

I told Mrs. Miles about how the tree that owns itself is a big fake. But she just smiled. She said she knew all along it was just a charming story. She said that's how a lot of history is. Part truth and part fake, all mixed together.

Some of the kids thought I should get a new topic, but Mrs. Miles said the tree is still a famous Athens place. So I decided to do my project about it.

Well, here's the true story: This history professor named E. Merton Coulter did a lot of research about the tree. Then he wrote an article in the *Georgia Historical Quarterly*. My mom helped me read it. (It's pretty long and complicated.)

He says the tree that owns itself was first mentioned in a newspaper article on August 12, 1890. Nobody signed the article. But the editor of the newspaper, the *Athens Banner*, was T. Larry Gantt.

Coulter couldn't find any deed or will about the tree. There was a Professor William Jackson who had kids, lived in Athens near the tree for a while, and died in Macon. He was buried in Athens in 1875. There wasn't anything about the tree in his obituary. Coulter looked in lots of books about famous places and trees. But this tree wasn't mentioned anywhere after Jackson died until fifteen years later, when the article came out in the *Athens Banner*. Then it wasn't mentioned anywhere again for another eleven years. So Coulter thinks the 1890 article was a joke meant to challenge the law students at the university. Make them think: could a tree really own itself?

In 1901, the *Athens Banner* put out a Centennial Edition. The tree story was in it again. Other writers started using the story in books. I guess they believed it was true. My dad says people believe anything they see in print.

Anyway, the tree that owns itself became famous. And the story about William Jackson became a legend. There is a little truth to it. Mr. Jackson did live near the tree for a few years. And the tree is a real thing. (Or the son of a real thing.) And people still visit it and write about it—like I'm doing.

Sunday night

I've been thinking about my project all weekend. I decided I'm proud of it. Sure, I'm doing my research on a sort of fake. But the story of the tree is interesting. It's different from plain, dull facts.

We studied tall tales in reading class. They're stories about real things that get exaggerated as they're retold. I guess the tree that owns itself is a "short" tale. It's a fictional story that became real as it was retold!

The tree really does own itself now. It's a famous place in Athens. Cars squeeze by it. The Athens Chamber of Commerce gives out information about it. Teachers assign projects about it. It was written up in *Ripley's Believe It Or Not*. Nobody is going to cut it down now. That would be unpatriotic!

And, in a way, the real story about the tree is neater than the legend. It shows you can make something true by believing it. When I told my dad the story, he grinned. He said it proved the pen is mightier than the sword. Get it? The legend of the tree that owns itself was written in ink. But now no sword can cut down the tree. I guess I'm glad I did my research on this famous place, after all.

Dear Jason,

I love your project. You discovered how research really works: you peel off layer after layer until you find the truth. If you try to take a shortcut, you may never understand what really happened!

Even though you were discouraged about your project, you decided to stick with it. I was very proud of you. And I agree with you. Some wonderful stories of our past are not 100 percent factual. We can enjoy the tale of the tree as a lovely legend. And we can learn a lot by understanding its true story.

I think you also learned the rewards of a job well done; you feel proud of yourself and your work. And I am putting a great big A plus by your name in my grade book. Congratulations!

Mrs. Miles

HISTORY IS ALL AROUND US

The tree that owns itself and the other famous landmarks mentioned are authentic places in Athens, Georgia. But there never was a child named Jason Jackson who wrote this journal. The information Jason learned when he tried to research the tree that owns itself is the same information the author learned when she researched the spot. This is not a true story, but the lessons Jason learned are true!

Another important Georgia tree, a live oak in Brunswick, Georgia, called the "Lover's Oak," is one of the oldest in the state. A historical marker certifies that this tree was alive when the Constitution was signed. The live oak is the official state tree of Georgia.

GEORGIA'S STRONG MAN

"The patient, Paul Anderson, still has a 104-degree temperature," the nurse said. She jotted something on a paper attached to a clipboard. "Delirium. Inner ear infection. Loss of weight," she continued. "Should I note anything else, Doctor?"

"Wish I knew what else," he muttered. "If we only knew what all he had, we might have a chance of getting him well in time. As it stands now, there is no way I can allow a man in his condition to compete."

Paul Anderson could hear the voices talking quietly. Where was he? He saw suitcases stacked by the door. He recognized them. There was his duffel bag with the AAU Weightlifting Team emblem on the side. Then he remembered. The 1956 Olympics in Melbourne, Australia. He had been training for months for this meet.

The doctor spoke directly to Paul. "Mr. Anderson, we must think about your health. You would be much better off back in the United States where you would be close to home. One thing we know you have is an inner ear infection. Surely you realize what a problem that would cause with your balance if you were to try to compete." The doctor took the newspaper from under his arm and laid it on Paul's bed. "I read the papers, too. I know how badly you want to stay."

Paul heard a third voice. "No publicity, Doctor. We absolutely don't want word of his illness to get around." He couldn't place the voice. The door closed quietly. Paul was left alone.

Paul picked up the *Herald-Sun*. Right on the front page was his photograph. It had been taken the year before at Gorky Park in front of a crowd of 15,000 Russians. He tried to focus his eyes to read the caption under his picture. Finally, he succeeded.

"The Russian audience called American heavyweight lifter Paul Anderson a 'Wonder of Nature' at Gorky Park last year at the USA/USSR dual team friendship meet in Moscow after he broke three world records in weight lifting. Lucky for us he has to make the long trip here to pick up his gold medal!"

Paul lay back on the pillow and closed his eyes. The Gorky Park meet had happened only a year ago, but it seemed like ten years ago now. And to think, he almost didn't get to go to Russia! Bob Hoffman, coach of the United States AAU weight lifting team, had planned to take Norbert Schemansky, the "Detroit Flash," to Russia. But Schemansky had been unable to go because of an old back injury and the team had expected to go without a heavyweight. Paul chuckled to himself. That was when he had volunteered, passport in hand.

Paul could just imagine Coach Hoffman's amazement when he got those telegrams from different cities throughout the United States. The telegrams were his friends' idea. They had asked their many trucker friends to send telegrams from all over the country urging Hoffman to give Paul the place on the team. He remembered how excited the guys were with their plan. "Come on, Little Atlas, it'll look like you've got nationwide support!" "Little Atlas" was their nickname for Paul. He could still see Harold Tanner and the others with their heads together as they plotted their strategy, just like in study hall back at Toccoa High School.

The door opened and Paul's teammate Mac entered. "How're you doin'?"

The concern in Mac's voice contrasted sharply with his casual question.

"They just gave me an injection. I think it's starting to take effect," Paul replied. "You don't have any aspirin, do you? I need to get over to the gym and train."

Mac shook his head in amazement. "Good grief, Paul! Don't you ever give up? I hate to tell you this, but they're not only talking about not letting you lift, they're talking about sending you back to the United States immediately! They can't figure out what you've got."

Paul shrugged his massive shoulders. "I'll refuse to leave. As long as there's any chance of my winning the gold medal, I'm going to stay right here. I can lift more when I'm sick than anybody else can when they're healthy! Now, will you get me some aspirin or not?"

Mac's lips tightened. Ignoring the question, he picked up the *Herald-Sun*. He pointed to Paul's photo. "That was some trip! The whole country was excited that the United States weight lifting team was going behind the Iron Curtain. That was about as thrilling as when General MacArthur's men made that daring landing on Inchon Harbor during the Korean War! I went to the same movie five times just to see the newsreels of the team. And you were the star! You were on right after Elvis Presley!" Mac's eyes skimmed the caption. "Who called you a 'Wonder of Nature'?"

Paul smiled briefly. "Those Russians were so impressed by strength, particularly by the strength of the heavyweights. Their guy had lifted his personal best of just over 330 pounds and tied a record. The crowd went wild. Then it was my turn. The Russians thought a last-minute fill-in like me didn't have a chance. Why, I didn't even have a uniform!"

Mac was so caught up in the story that he barely noticed that Paul's voice seemed to be getting stronger.

"When I asked for 402 ½ pounds, the crowd laughed. After all, they had never even heard of Paul Anderson. And the world record was 360 pounds. The audience couldn't believe it when I actually lifted forty-two pounds over the record."

"I guess the crowd got excited all over again," Mac said.

"Did they ever! They were standing on their chairs and throwing their hats." Paul's voice regained its booming quality as he relived his memories. "People were shouting that I was a 'Wonder of Nature.' That's when this very old man came to the platform with his interpreter. The old man announced that he could go home and die now because he had seen everything there was to see."

"Guess you know the Russians aren't even entering anyone in the heavyweight division here," Mac said. "You must've scared them off completely! The heavyweights that are entered thought they were only competing for second place. Believe me, they've got their hopes up now!"

"But they don't know about my illness," Paul protested.

"Word has leaked out." Mac placed the newspaper back on Paul's bed. "Tomorrow's write-up won't be as positive as this." He rose to leave.

"The aspirin?" Paul asked again.

Mac looked at him sympathetically. "If your doctor wanted you to have aspirin, he'd be giving it to you."

"Aw, come on. I know myself better than he does. It always brings my fever down," Paul said.

Mac slowly nodded. "Be back in a few minutes."

The morning dawned clear and bright in Melbourne, Australia. Paul opened his eyes. It was November 25, 1956. This was the big day. Paul reached for his aspirin bottle. Because his fever was down, the team physician said he would allow Paul to lift in competition, but only if Paul took responsibility for any ill effects on his health. Paul agreed immediately.

Paul was nearly two weeks behind with his training for the 1956 Olympic weight lifting event. What a total reverse of his training philosophy! Like Milo, the Greek weight lifter who had lifted a cow every day from the time she was a small calf until she was fully grown, Paul had always believed in a gradual training program. As a teenager he had even tried to duplicate Milo's training method. He put his pony, Old Dan, in a fence in his own backyard, and every day he would attempt to hoist the surprised animal off the ground. Old Dan was a great pony, but he just never understood why Paul wanted to lift him.

Finally, Paul left Old Dan on the ground and developed other methods of training. How many junkyards had he and his dad gone to? He still had those huge iron wheels attached to that steel rod. When Paul could handle that weight, they went to still more junkyards to find heavy items to hang on the iron wheels. When he outgrew those weights, they filled two fifty-five gallon barrels with concrete. They were attached by chains to a bar he placed over his shoulders. Paul would lift them, one on each side!

The heavyweights were scheduled to lift at 8:00 P.M. Paul arrived on time, but the competition was running about five hours behind schedule. The heavyweights, as always, were the last to compete.

Paul entered the arena and stepped up to the scale. He still looked like a mountain of a man, but somehow paler and less imposing now. He rubbed his eyes as he stared at the scale. Surely his vision was blurred! The scale read 304 pounds. Paul had weighed 340 pounds when he arrived in Melbourne. He couldn't believe that he had lost so much weight during his illness!

At midnight, the competition was still going on. The effects of the aspirin had worn off, and Paul's fever was raging again. It would be at least another hour before he would lift. Why hadn't he brought the aspirin bottle? Paul knew the answer even as he asked. He had thought the meet would be over by now. He was dizzy, sweating, and shivering all at the same time.

Paul was introduced at one o'clock in the morning. He removed his sweatsuit and managed to reach the lifting platform without collapsing. For his first lift, the "press," he chose only a warm-up weight. He couldn't believe how heavy it seemed! He tried to regain his old rhythm. He had mentally practiced the lift time and time again as he lay in his hospital bed. Raise the barbell from the floor to shoulder level. Raise it overhead. Pause. By talking himself through the "press" Paul was able to complete it successfully.

Paul had two more chances to improve his score for the "press." He increased the weights, knowing he could not win a gold medal with his warm-up weight. Partway into both lifts, he realized he could not complete them! The weights crashed to the floor. Paul was horrified! His illness had sapped his strength. Two weeks ago these weights would have been easy.

Paul could barely see. It took extraordinary self-discipline for him to stay conscious for the next event, the "snatch." Over and over he focused on the movements. Brace. Balance. Lift the barbell from the floor to over his head in one uninterrupted movement. But how difficult that would be with his inner ear infection!

Remembering his earlier strategy, Paul again started with a weight he ordinarily could handle easily. He staggered, nearly dropping the barbell. Then he managed to drive it successfully overhead. He tried slightly heavier weights for the next two lifts. But once again he could not complete the second and third tries. It was obvious to the other lifters that Paul Anderson was in trouble.

The results were tallied. The combined weight of each contestant's best lifts determined his score. As Paul entered the third event, the "clean and jerk," he was behind. He had never faced that situation before. His performance had been so poor it was giving the other lifters new hope. A wide smile spread across Humberto

Selvetti's face, and he flexed his biceps until they bulged.

The other lifters were nearly panting, eager for their turns. To Paul they looked like a pack of dogs baring their teeth and coming in for the final kill. They seemed to attack the barbells, beating their personal records with each try.

Paul had no reason to believe he would be any more successful with the "clean and jerk" than he had been with the "press" or the "snatch." Yet, being this close, he could not quit now. Years of preparation had gone into this day, and he was determined to forge ahead. He gripped his head till his knuckles were white. He had to lie down.

Paul found a place to sleep on a cot behind the lifting platform. He asked an Australian aide to awaken him when it was his turn. He was exhausted, but his sleep was fitful. His anxiety was visible even as he slept.

At 3:00 A.M., the Australian shook Paul.

"Feeling any better?" he asked.

Paul's glazed eyes looked past the Australian as he shook his head numbly. "How's the meet going?" he mumbled.

The Australian spoke very slowly. "I regret having to tell you this. To win the gold medal you will have to lift an Olympic record of 414 ½ pounds. You would need that amount to make up for your first two events. If you lift 414 ½ pounds, you will tie Humberto Selvetti of Argentina. He is your closest competitor. You now weigh twelve pounds less than Selvetti. That lift would give you the gold medal in a tie, according to Olympic rules."

Paul had lifted 440 pounds in competition before. Of course, that was when he was healthy. But, now, 414 ½ pounds sounded like the weight of an elephant to him. What should he do? Ask for the higher weight and risk failing in front of everyone? Try for a silver or a bronze? Paul maneuvered himself out of the cot. With a huge effort, he hoisted himself to an upright position. He inched his way toward the lifting platform. *The clean and jerk,* he said to himself. *Pull the barbell up to my chest. Pause. Jerk it overhead.*

Paul finally reached the platform. "Give me 414 ½ pounds," he said.

The hall was silent as the official placed the weights on the bar. With a deep breath, Paul picked up the barbell from the floor. He got it as high as his chest. Bracing himself, he gave it an upward thrust but got it only as high as his chin. The barbell seemed to be alive, to have a mind of its own, almost like Old Dan the pony as he struggled to get away. Paul could not complete the lift. The hall rang with the echoes of the barbell as it hit the floor.

Tension in the hall crackled. Paul's teammates surrounded him, slapped him on the back, and showered him with words of encouragement. These athletes had never seen him fail. They could not believe it could happen. Paul had three minutes to rest before his next attempt. He had to try again. He owed it to his teammates.

On his second try, Paul's enthusiasm evaporated as soon as he got the bar to his chest. The barbell seemed to have gained weight during the past three minutes. Again it fell clanging to the floor. His frustration was almost unbearable. He waved his teammates away. There was no way he could face them.

Paul walked away from the arena. He found himself in a dark adjoining hallway. He was a religious man, but when he tried to pray, he felt awkward and out of practice.

Paul closed his eyes and saw the faces of his family. He could picture his dad the day they had put the weights and chains in the huge oak tree in his back yard. His dad had insisted on digging the hole in the hard-packed earth where Paul would stand under the chains. "These aren't the muscles you need to strengthen," he told Paul, throwing a shovelful of dirt over his shoulder. His mother had prepared countless nutritious meals to help him build his strength. "Eat up, and never give up." He thought of his sister Dot. She had always shared everything with him, even her precious piano. Paul finally had convinced her that for him piano lessons were a lost cause. Dot was the musician and he was the weight lifter.

Dot and her husband had shared their home with Paul during his last year at Toccoa High School. He still remembered those barbells and that stack of *Strength and Health* magazines in the bedroom. His brother-in-law Julius had long been interested in weight lifting. Why, he had taken a year off work in order to travel with Paul and chauffeur him to many celebrity events!

Paul thought of his friends. He remembered Bob Peoples, an athlete well-known among weight lifters, who had written the first story to appear about Paul. He pictured his friend Fred, who had always found Paul's strength amazing. Once Paul could not get out of his parking place at the Lone Oak restaurant because a car was blocking his way. Fred had roared with amazed laughter when Paul picked up the car and moved it.

Paul thought of the upcoming moment for his teammates who still did not believe he could be defeated. Supported by these

expectant faces of family, friends, and teammates, Paul returned to the arena. He mounted the lifting platform for his final lift in the "clean and jerk" event.

Paul bent down and grasped the barbell. Using all his strength, he got the weight up to his chest. There it stayed, as though frozen in place. He thought of the safe back in Toccoa that he had filled with cement for lifting practice. One night it had frozen to the ground, and Paul could not budge it. Surely this lift would be just as impossible. Hadn't it been useless to attempt to lift the entire frozen backyard where the safe was anchored?

Paul felt a warmth spreading throughout his chest. It was unlike any sensation he could remember. Suddenly he started to pray. This time, it was straight from the heart. "No deals, God. But don't you think you could help me get this up over my head?" Had he spoken the words aloud? He wasn't sure.

Paul bent his knees slightly to gain added momentum for the final thrust. He pushed the weight overhead and held it steady. After a moment of astonished silence, the sound of cheering engulfed the arena. Paul brought the bar down to the floor. He had done it! He had won the 1956 Olympic gold medal in the heavyweight division! But in his heart Paul Anderson knew he had not won this victory alone.

MORE ABOUT GEORGIA'S STRONG MAN

Paul Anderson, the Georgia athlete, is still listed in the Guinness Book of World Records as the world's strongest man. He lifted 6,270 pounds with his back in 1957. During his career, he broke many world records in weight lifting.

In spite of failing health in his later years, Paul Anderson and his wife Glenda founded and ran the Paul Anderson Youth Home in Vidalia, Georgia. They reared their daughter, Paula Anderson Schaefer, on its beautiful campus. The youth home operates its own school and accepts as many as twenty homeless or troubled youth at a time. More than 2,000 young men have lived there and gone on to lead productive lives. Many people think of Paul Anderson as a great athlete and an even greater humanitarian.

MAX, THE PARATROOPING DOG

"Jump!" The deep voice thundered.

Max jumped through the door of the plane into midair. He looked up toward the jumpers still in the plane. His rust-brown hair was standing straight up as though at attention. Max looked down and saw the ground coming up fast below him. Then the white silk parachute billowed out, slowing his fall. Max jerked his head upward to watch. As though responding to the "at ease" command, Max's hair again lay flat. All around him, the breezes were cluttered with shouts of encouragement. The soldiers of Fort Benning's 505th Parachute Infantry Regiment were proud of him!

Once on the ground, Max stood calmly. The other jumpers ran up to him to unfasten his harnesses and collapse his chute.

"Hey, Max! Wasn't that first step a doozy?"

"Maxie-Boy, you made a four-point landing!"

"What a dog! Max, the Germans don't have a boxer that can hold a candle to you!"

The attention continued that night in the barracks. The soldiers were busy packing their chutes for the next day. But not one soldier in the barracks missed a chance to scratch behind Max's ears or to give him a treat.

"You sure didn't freeze up, Buddy," said Clyde. "Spacing between the jumpers was just right!"

"You know, that's right!" James answered, tightening the buckle on his chute. "Max didn't even interrupt the timing pattern when he jumped out."

"Wow, if those girl dogs could've seen you today!" Several other soldiers laughed and walked over.

"And that four-point landing! It's all I can do to keep my balance on two legs!"

"That's some dog you got there, Gray. Ain't no other unit anywhere's got a mascot like him!" The other men nodded vigorously.

"Pretty obvious he feels like he belongs to all of us," James Gray responded with a smile.

"Weren't you worried about whether he could do it?" Clyde Russell asked.

"A little. I sure thought about it. Course it would've broken even that tough heart of his if he hadn't gotten to come."

"Yeah, I know." Clyde lifted Max's chin with his hand and looked into his soft brown eyes. "But still, jumpin' from a plane isn't the same as jumpin' from the control tower."

"Well, Max already knew how it felt to jump. And he knew to keep his legs relaxed when he landed." James looked thoughtful. "Of course, jumping from the doorway of a moving plane is a pretty big step."

"And then when he felt that jerk as the parachute opened! Did he ever look surprised!" Clyde laughed as he rubbed Max's head.

Max just yawned. Unfazed by the bantering, Max curled up beside James Gray's bunk and went to sleep.

After lights out, Clyde Russell said in a low voice, "Max, you dreamin' about jumpin'?"

Every man in the barracks fell asleep chuckling.

The next day Max was up at the first note of reveille. As usual, he wanted to go along with his friends. He had worked with them every step of the way, from the early training on the ground to yesterday's jump. In this fourth and final week, all their training would be put to the test.

Max's favorite training maneuver had been the rugged cross-country running. In times of war, paratroopers must know what to do when they hit the ground or they would make easy targets for the enemy. As soon as they touch down, the jumpers must run to cover quickly. If they don't, the enemy could simply watch them land and capture or shoot them on the spot. Naturally, Max did not realize this. He just knew he loved to run, and running was more fun when his people ran with him.

Max trotted from one soldier to another in the barracks uttering his short, sharp, questioning barks.

"We wouldn't leave without you, Max. Especially not now that you've proven yourself. Wouldn't be as exciting if you weren't there!"

Max heard the welcoming tone of voice. He showed his elation by furiously wagging his tail. He took off running out the open door of the barracks, made a turn around the flagpole, and ran back inside the barracks. Max had been gone less than thirty seconds. With his tail thumping the wooden floor, he sat and watched every move the soldiers made as they prepared their gear. They carried their equipment outside while Max danced alongside.

Max stopped his dance in midstep when he heard the roar of the transport plane. He realized this meant another jump from the plane. His tail suddenly stopped wagging, and his whole body stiffened. This time Max resisted boarding the transport plane with all of his ninety pounds. With a whimper he begged to stay on the ground.

"Max, you know you'd hate it if we left without you." James's voice had its usual calming effect. Max's ears lifted in response to his master's voice. He took a step forward. James and Clyde quickly lifted Max inside the plane. Clyde hooked Max into his harness.

The plane roared down the runway and lifted into the air. The atmosphere was tense. The soldiers sat silently with their backs against the outside wall of the transport plane and awaited the jump master's move. Most paratroopers find their second jump to be the most difficult. They know what they have to do and how hard it is. They have also had time to realize all the things that might go wrong. And the second jump is just not as much of a thrill as the first one.

"Stand up and hook up!" Even the jump master's voice betrayed a slight edge of nervousness.

All the men stood and hooked their parachutes onto the static line. Max stood, too. His legs were quivering. Clyde Russell attached Max's parachute. He slipped him a biscuit he had saved from his own breakfast.

"Check equipment," the jump master's commanding voice sounded again.

Each man checked the equipment of the man standing in line ahead of him. After he examined the gear of the paratrooper in front of him, James carefully checked Max's parachute.

"Count off."

"One," yelled the first man in line.

"Two," called out James.

There was a slight pause. "Three," Clyde answered for Max. A ripple of nervous laughter broke the tension momentarily. Max tilted his head toward the voices of each of his friends as they counted off.

The jump master lifted his hand to signal the pilot. The plane slowed and drifted slightly toward earth.

The door was pushed aside. "Stand in the door," came the command. The men started their procession.

Then the awaited command rang out like a pistol shot.

"Go!"

The first man leaped out the door. Almost as one voice, the men on board counted out, "One thousand, two thousand, three thousand." They breathed a sigh of relief as the static line opened the parachute. Then they heard the command for the second jump.

"Go!"

Now it was Max's turn. His legs trembled. He sniffed the doorway of the airplane. He turned to go back but was blocked by the paratroopers behind him in line. Everyone tried to help.

"Just like you did yesterday, Max."

"About like the movin' trucks we jumped out of last week."

There was a chuckle. "Well, a little higher up!"

"Come on, Max. Would it help if I threw a sirloin steak out the door first?"

Someone laughed. "That'd give him something to go after."

"Just pretend it's another training tower jump, Max. That's what I'm going to do." The soldier's voice sounded shaky as he tried to laugh.

"Go!" The jump master's voice barked his command.

Max abruptly jumped into the immense space under him. The paratroopers in the plane above him could hear his mournful wail as he plunged toward the ground. His parachute opened like a huge white umbrella. The men cheered. Max swung on toward the field below. All eyes were on him as he again made a four-point landing.

One by one, other paratroopers followed Max in perfect formation as they drifted toward their target. This time one soldier started singing on his way down. "You're in the Army now. You're not behind a plow. You'll never get rich, a-diggin' a ditch. You're in the Army now." The others joined in.

Max gazed up into the sky dotted with the white parachutes

of the 505th. He perked up his ears as the men's voices reached him. Then he lifted his chin and joined in with a howl.

Max was still howling as the other jumpers swarmed around him. They unhooked his harness and took care of his chute.

"Always have to do what we do, don't ya, Buddy?"

"You do need to work on your singing, though!" James laughed.

"His singing is perfect!" Max's regiment was loyal to their mascot.

Max performed this jump three more times. Forgetting his reluctance on the second jump, Max now entered the transport plane eagerly. He maintained his record of perfect four-point landings.

By December 1, 1942, Max had completed five jumps from a plane in flight. He had parachuted from a height of at least 800 feet. He had landed each time without injury. This made him the first dog ever to qualify as a paratrooper.

Max's day in the spotlight soon arrived. A review was staged in his honor. All the men of the 505th Parachute Infantry Regiment at Fort Benning, Georgia, stood at attention in full dress uniform. Max was dressed for the occasion in a small cloth jacket. Colonel James Gavin solemnly pinned the silver wings to Max's jacket. The wings signified he was now a paratrooper. As if on cue, Max lifted his paw for the colonel to shake. There was a burst of applause. Max had become the first certified dog paratrooper.

Max's fame grew. He continued to train, making three more jumps in December, 1942. Three newsreel companies asked to film Max making his jumps. Before dawn on December 17, 1942, the very day the filming was to take place, Max was making his early morning rounds of the army base. Just as he stepped into the street, Max was hit by a speeding two-ton truck.

Max was badly injured. In fact, the surgeons of the 505th thought he would die. Still, the veterinarians set his broken bones and wired up his shattered jaw. They even gave him intravenous feedings to supply extra energy. Pictures of the injured dog ran in newspapers throughout the country. There was an outburst of interest and sympathy for Max from all over the United States. Max received so many cards and letters that Staff Sergeant Harry E. Anderson volunteered to serve as Max's correspondence secretary. People sent money to help pay for Max's care. A surgeon sent instructions for a new splint. An artist wrote asking to paint Max's picture to put in a series he was painting called "Dogs in Defense." The children at Fort Benning school sent Max a decorated Christmas tree.

Max's recovery was not smooth. He was not used to splints, wires, needles, and gauze bandages. Early in January, he managed to paw off and swallow eight yards of gauze bandages. The Army surgeons came to Max's rescue once again. They had to open his abdomen to remove all the gauze. No one had expected Max to have to fight that battle. He lost about twenty pounds.

Max's mail kept coming. Other dogs sent messages to Max through their masters and mistresses. Sergeant Anderson answered all the letters for Max and even wrote some of his own, signing Max's name at the bottom. Once Anderson read about a showgirl in Kansas City who had broken her leg. Through Sergeant Anderson, Max asked the girl to send a picture, and in return he promised to send her a picture of himself.

Max finally was released from the Veterinarian's Hospital on February 11, 1943. He had been in the hospital nearly two months. Max's jaw was still bandaged to keep him from gnawing on hard bones. Chewing bones might injure his jaw again.

But even with a bandaged jaw, Max wagged his stubby tail enthusiastically as he received another promotion. His owner, Major James Gray, read the papers of his promotion. Then he pinned the Master Sergeant stripes on Max's jacket. That same day Max was awarded the Wounded in Action decoration.

Soon after Max was released from the hospital, he left Fort Benning, Georgia. He went with the members of the 505th Parachute Infantry Regiment to Camp Hofman, North Carolina. The children of Fort Benning were sad to see their famous friend leave. So Max left something behind for Georgians to remember him by. On February 18, 1943, the Fort Benning newspaper printed photographs of Max and Mrs. Max with their litter of six puppies. Each puppy was an exact, miniature copy of Paratrooper Max.

MORE ABOUT DOGS IN THE UNITED STATES ARMED FORCES

Max's story is true. Max was a boxer, but dogs of many breeds served with the U.S. armed forces during World War II. Many, like Max, served as mascots to improve morale. Others played a more active role in the defense of our country. Many lives were saved by dogs trained as scouts who could spot the enemy before they could open fire. These scout dogs would growl and go on point to warn their soldiers. The Army found that a sentry dog could do the job of six to eight men when guarding tanks and airplanes at night. With their keen sense of smell, sentry dogs could detect intruders far sooner than a human could. Dogs also served as messengers during World War II. They carried messages to the front lines, all the while dodging shells and enemy fire. Then the messenger dogs risked their lives again as they carried another message back to headquarters.

GONE BUT NOT FORGOTTEN

The smoke from the Gypsies' campfire drifted up through the early morning fog. Autumn mornings in Athens always excited Harriet because that was when the Gypsies arrived and turned her little northeastern Georgia town into a Spanish countryside. She could hear the rapid staccato of the Gypsies' voices. So many voices, from the deep basses of the men to the high-pitched melodies of the children.

Harriet looked through the trees at their campground. Their wagons, decorated in brilliant colors of orange, red, and yellow, formed a circle around the Gypsy campfire. Small, dark-haired children were scurrying back and forth between the trailers and the fire. Their brightly colored clothes glowed as they ran about, stopping now and then to collect wood for kindling. They reminded Harriet of cardinals and goldfinches finding twigs to build their nests.

Harriet smiled. This was almost as good as visiting another country. If only she had her paints and some free time. What a sight to capture on canvas!

A rush of dark fur flew at Harriet. She threw up her arms to shield her face. Then something heavy gripped her around the neck and waist. She teetered, trying to keep her balance.

Harriet found herself nose to nose with a large monkey. She struggled to loosen the furry grasp. The animal's teeth were chattering. The two bells dangling from his red collar jingled wildly. The monkey was every bit as scared as she was!

Two boys came running toward Harriet. She frowned, recognizing the faces of her classmates. The boys were out of breath, sweating. She knew at once they had been chasing the monkey. She wasn't surprised. These boys were just the type who would think it was great sport to chase after someone's pet. But, whose pet was it? No one around here had a monkey. Suddenly, it came to her. The monkey must be a Gypsy pet!

"You've scared him to death!" she yelled at them. "Why'd you do that?"

"Aw, we were just playin' with him. We didn't hurt him none." Robert held out his arms to take the monkey. "Come on, give him back." Robert grinned, trying to look harmless. The monkey tightened his choke hold on Harriet's neck.

"Give him back? You never had him," Harriet pointed out.

"Give him to me, girl. Or we'll make you sorry." Robert's grin had changed to a sneer. "Real sorry. Won't we, Jim?"

"Hey, Robert, we better git goin'. If I git another tardy, my ol' man's gonna send me to reform school." Jim seemed to be losing interest in Harriet and the monkey.

"Why do you care? You wouldn't have to go to school. Just think of the neat things you could teach yourself." Robert snickered at his own joke.

"I suppose you taught yourself how to be cruel to animals!" Harriet held her breath. Would they let that remark pass?

Jim ignored her and took a step away. "Let's go," he said.

Robert looked again at Harriet. "You goin' to school or playin' nursemaid?" he taunted as they turned to go.

Harriet didn't bother to answer. She patted the monkey to calm him down. Then she tried to unwind his arms and legs from her body, but the more she pulled, the tighter he clung. Finally, she loosened his grip enough to set him on the ground. But as soon as she let go, he jumped back into her arms. She looked around for some help. The boys were already out of sight. Now she would be late for school, too!

With her heart pounding, Harriet started toward the Gypsy camp. Suddenly the monkey let out a squeal. He jumped from her arms and tore off through the trees. A Gypsy girl about fourteen appeared at the edge of the woods. Her full red skirt looked like a giant poppy.

The monkey flew straight into the girl's arms. She threw her arms around him, chattering excitedly in strange words. She seemed to alternate between scolding and rejoicing. The girl looked cautiously over her shoulder before walking closer to Harriet.

As she stepped forward to meet the Gypsy girl, Harriet stepped in a hole and went sprawling.

"Let me help you," the girl said in clear English. "Are you hurt?"

Harriet shook her head, rubbing her ankle. Her cheeks burned. The monkey placed his face directly in front of Harriet's face. He

touched her chin with his tiny finger and grunted as if he were asking how she was. Harriet smiled, forgetting her embarrassment.

The Gypsy girl's eyes sparkled with amusement and lit up her entire face. "I think she's just fine, Dizzy," she said. "And you'd better thank her. I wonder where you'd be right now if she hadn't come along." Dizzy hopped down from the girl's arms, bowed from the waist, and handed Harriet a pencil.

"Where'd you get that? That's my pencil!" Harriet yelped.

Dizzy jumped up and down and cackled.

"You stole my pencil!" Harriet accused.

Dizzy hung his head and put his hands over his face.

"Oh, no," the Gypsy girl said. "He doesn't steal. He just finds things that aren't lost." Her eyes twinkled again.

Harriet stroked Dizzy's brown fur. "They really scared you, didn't they, fella?" Dizzy thrust out a long arm and patted the cornrows on Harriet's head.

Harriet looked at the Gypsy girl. "You must have seen those boys chase your monkey. I don't know why they are so mean sometimes."

The Gypsy girl smiled at Harriet. Then she spoke sharply to Dizzy. The monkey covered his eyes with one hand. Peeking through his fingers, he drew Harriet's blue hair ribbon from behind his back.

Harriet giggled, "I see you found something else that wasn't lost!" She beckoned Dizzy with her finger. The monkey held out the ribbon stiffly. Harriet took it from his hand and tied it in a bow on his collar. The monkey threw back his head and clapped.

"Nation, Nation!" shouted a voice in the distance. The shout was followed by a waterfall of words in the same language Harriet had heard before.

"*Dae*," the Gypsy girl called back. Then she turned to Harriet. "Listen, I saw what you did—standing up to those *bengs*, you know, boys! Come back after school, and I'll give you something. Meet you here!" She flashed Harriet a brilliant smile. Harriet noticed that the gold coins braided into the Gypsy girl's hair seemed to throw off sparks as she ran through the patches of sunlight.

School dragged for Harriet. She doodled through her lessons. What was the matter with her today? Not even her drawings looked right. She drew several pictures of the morning adventure, but she threw them all away except the one of Nation and Dizzy returning her pencil. She finished by labeling the bottom of the picture: October 19, 1921, Linton's Grove, Athens, Georgia. It had certainly been a day to remember!

Harriet began walking home. Oh, no! Not Jim and Robert again!

They jeered, "We thought you'd spend the day with the Gypsies! Don't you know they steal kids?" In a singsong voice they chanted together:

"My mother said I never should
Play with the Gypsies in the wood."

Unable to get past them, Harriet marched back into the schoolhouse. Jim and Robert followed her all the way to the door. Safe inside, she waited until they left. Then she headed for the Gypsy campground.

Harriet took a deep breath as she started through the trees.

Suddenly, Nation stepped out from behind a red oak tree. She had been waiting! Harriet felt a flood of relief. Then she stared. Nation was wearing eight bracelets, four coin necklaces, and some wire hoop earrings. She wore a bright yellow shawl around her shoulders and the same poppy skirt. She whirled once before she offered her hand in greeting.

Harriet drank in the swirling blend of colors. "I'm Harriet Brooks. I live over there just beyond the campground."

"I'm Carnation Carroll." The Gypsy girl grinned. "Where I am living depends on what time of year it is."

Harriet looked at her curiously, "Do you like moving so often?"

"Well, I got to meet you," Nation pointed out. "That never would have happened if I hadn't come to Athens."

Harriet smiled at Nation. Fleetingly she wondered if she should be there.

As though reading her mind, Nation asked, "Do your parents know you're here?"

"No," Harriet admitted.

"I won't be saying anything to my folks, either," Nation said. She led the way deeper into the woods.

"Don't Gypsies like other folks comin' around?" Harriet asked.

"Don't say Gypsies! We call ourselves Travelers," Nation said.

Harriet's forehead wrinkled. "What's wrong with the word 'Gypsy'?"

Nation glanced at her impatiently. "We just don't like it. Maybe at one time Gypsy was okay. But now we're Travelers, it describes us better."

"Is that why your folks don't like us comin' around, 'cause we call you Gypsies?" Harriet asked.

"No, it's because most times when people come around, it's to accuse us of taking something. But we don't take what we don't need." Nation's black eyes flashed.

"And," Nation said as though reading Harriet's thoughts, "we definitely don't steal *Gadjo* children. We have enough of our own!" She laughed with merriment.

Nation reached into the fork of a tree just above Harriet's eye level. She brought down a small, beautifully made willow basket. Harriet turned the dainty basket over in her hands.

"I made it for you," said Nation.

"It's lovely!" Harriet said. "I could never make anything like this. It must take a very long time to make something this fine."

"I learned it from my *familia*," Nation said proudly.

"I brought you something, too," Harriet said, taking out the picture she had drawn of Nation and Dizzy.

Nation gasped. "Amazing! Anyone in the clan would know this was Dizzy and me. You even drew his bell collar and my long braids. And you say you couldn't make a basket!"

Nation pointed to the words and numbers under the picture. "What does it say?" she asked.

"Can't you read?" Harriet blurted out.

Nation pointed to the date. "That says October."

"Don't you go to school?" Harriet asked in surprise.

"Not too often. Lots of schooling would make us too much like the *Gadjo*."

"How do you learn then?"

"We can learn all we need to know from our *familia*," Nation explained. "I can only read and write a few of your *Gadjo* words. But, I can read fortunes—lots of them. Want me to read yours?"

"Can you do it right now?" Harriet asked.

Nation nodded. "Do you like my *diklo*?" she asked, rearranging her shawl to cover her hair. "That's Romani for scarf. I borrowed it from my sister, Ritsy, the fortune-teller. She tells people what they want or don't want to hear. I learned to tell fortunes from listening to Ritsy."

Nation motioned for Harriet to sit down on a nearby log. Nation sat beside her and placed Harriet's hand palm up on her lap. Then she looked searchingly into Harriet's eyes. "I see a lovely dark face looking at an easel which holds a canvas filled with colors."

Harriet barely breathed as she listened.

"As I look closer at the painting, I can see the canvas contains the faces of many different kinds of jungle animals. I see a lion and a monkey. Maybe you were remembering Dizzy! The animals are all hiding. Their faces are only there if you search for them."

Harriet's eyes were glowing with excitement.

Nation abruptly dropped Harriet's hand.

"That's all I can see for free. Perhaps if you had a nickel..."

Harriet quickly pulled out a nickel. Nation barely glanced at it as she slipped it into her skirt. "I see other paintings, too. Some of them have ribbons on them. They must have won prizes. I might could see more if..." Nation held out her hand.

Harriet stood up. "I've got to go."

Nation looked at her steadily. "You are angry with me."

Harriet shrugged.

"I'll tell you more for free," Nation continued. "I see you watching a parade. It seems to be in honor of someone special. There are many Travelers there, along with their wagons, horses, and mules. You seem to be watching for someone special, maybe it's me! You watch until it is over and then you seem disappointed."

Harriet was silent.

"I'm going to tell you a Traveler's secret. If you come sometime and can't find me," she said, "look up there." Nation pointed to the fork of the tree where she had hidden Harriet's basket the day before. "We put our messages above eye level so a *Gadjo* won't see or touch."

Nation walked with Harriet to the edge of the trees. The girls turned toward the campground as the sounds of lively music began.

"Come back another day," Nation said. She began waving her arms in time to the music. Her poppy skirt flared out as she whirled. "I could teach you to dance the Flamenco." Nation's jewelry clinked together as she danced away, adding her own accents to the music as it filtered through the trees.

At breakfast the next morning, Harriet asked, "Dad, have you heard of the Travelers? Most folks call them Gypsies. They're staying over at Linton's Grove."

"Well, I know they come through in the fall. They paint barns for money. Usually, they make 'em red. Some folks say the paint rinses off in the first hard rain," Harriet's father said.

"Does it really rinse off?" Harriet asked.

"Never did, as far as I could tell. Anyway, I don't much like to be misjudged—don't guess they do either." Her father smiled at her over his newspaper.

"Do you think the Travelers cheat folks?" Harriet asked.

Her father laughed, "If they do cheat, nobody can ever prove it!"

Harriet sat quietly for a moment. "Hasn't anyone ever made you feel cheated?" Harriet persisted.

"Not more'n once," he said. "Not if I can help it."

"But what if this person was someone really fun?" Harriet asked. "Someone you wanted to get to know better. Would you give them another chance?"

"Yep, reckon I would," he said thoughtfully. "And then if it happened again, I'd have to decide if I was gettin' more than I was cheated out of."

Her father moved his chair back. "You seem mighty curious about the Gypsies. I heard about a big Gypsy funeral today in town. They come from all over." He looked at his watch. "Want to go? You might not have another chance to see something like that."

Nation's fortune-telling had been right. The funeral procession was like a big parade. It continued as far as Harriet could see. Harriet watched horses and mules pulling the most beautiful wagons she had ever seen. The wagons were decorated on the sides with plate glass mirrors which were interspersed with brightly painted scenes and carved wood. The wagons were four or five across, so the mirrored wagon sides reflected the paintings on the wagons on either side of them. Harriet felt like she was watching a carousel with no end, a kaleidoscope turned inside out.

Harriet spotted a large black wreath. The ribbon around it said, "gone but not forgotten." Harriet's father read the words aloud and told her that was what the Travelers carved into their tombstones.

After the last of the big wagons rolled slowly out of sight, Harriet and her father headed home. "Are their wagons that pretty inside?" Harriet asked.

"I think so," her father responded. "I do know they are painted and have some carved wood inside. They're really just bedrooms, you know. They cook outside."

The next morning Harriet awoke to the smell of smoke. She dressed quickly, went downstairs, then opened the front door to look out. She could see dark smoke rising above the trees of Linton's Grove. Banging the door shut, she took off running. She pushed her way through the others who were standing around the campground. She could see the charred remains of a burned trailer. Only some dishes and metal pans lay smoldering in the ashes. Nothing and no one else was left—no Nation, no Dizzy, no anyone! Who had done this? Was anyone hurt? Whose trailer was it? Where were the Travelers? The smoke stung Harriet's eyes.

Scraps of conversation from the crowd drifted into Harriet's mind. "Custom to burn their trailer when someone dies."

"Do it in the middle of the night."

"Guess they don't want to use anything that belonged to a dead person."

"We saw 'em pullin' out. Wasn't too long after the fire started."

And finally, "Guess them Gypsies won't be back till next fall, unless someone dies or gets married," said a man standing nearby.

Harriet turned and screamed, "They like to be called Travelers!" Several faces she recognized looked at her curiously.

What a drab scene! The whole picture seemed to be painted with shades of gray. What a contrast to the Travelers' colorful caravan!

Harriet wandered into the woods and sat on the fortune-telling log. She remembered the small willow basket. Harriet's gaze lifted to the tree branch where Nation had put the basket. She stood up and reached eagerly into the fork of the tree. There was a large roll of paper in it! Harriet unrolled it and pulled it open. It was a drawing of a girl and a monkey. Harriet recognized her own cornrows tied up with tiny ribbons. And there was the blouse she had worn the day she met Nation and Dizzy. The monkey was wearing a collar with two bells and tied with a ribbon. Harriet and Dizzy!

At the bottom of the picture, in perfect outline, were the words, "gone but not forgotten." The letters were beautifully formed, like the words on the chart at school. Had Nation been trying to fool her about not being able to read and write?

Harriet remembered the funeral wreath she had seen the day before. She thought of the remark she had heard about Travelers' tombstones. Why, Nation must have done a rubbing from one of the stone markers in the Oconee Hills Cemetery! She had gone to a lot of trouble to leave a message to a *Gadjo*—to Harriet! This was her message to Harriet! Harriet turned the big sheet of paper over.

Awkwardly formed letters and numbers spelled out October 20, 1921. Maybe this was Nation's way of saying, "Until next fall." Only then did the tears begin to roll down Harriet's cheeks.

MORE ABOUT THE TRAVELERS

For over half a century, a caravan of Travelers regularly traveled through Athens, Georgia. They were on the move throughout the spring, summer, and fall, remaining in one place during the winter. They often ordered new wagons to be made in Athens at the Klein-Martin Company, the only builders of wagons that Athens ever had. This company specialized in building wagons for the roving bands of Gypsies who traveled through Athens to trade horses and mules, do home repairs, and tell fortunes. They ordered wagons made to their specifications and then picked them up the following year.

Sometimes Gypsy funerals were held in Athens. The body was sent by train. After a long day of festivities extending far into the night, the deceased was buried in the Oconee Hills Cemetery.

KING OF THE SWAMP

One look at Obediah Barber and Edmond could tell he was mad. Why, his pa's mouth looked like a slit running from one side of his lean face to the other! And he didn't stop to say a word. Just took the wagon and went back to the swamp. That's how Edmond knew something was going on.

So Edmond followed along. His kid sister Ella tagged along, too. It wasn't hard keeping up on foot because the clumps of wiregrass slowed down the wheels of the wagon. Edmond didn't speak. Neither did Ella. They knew better than to pester at their pa. They just knew something was going on. Obediah would tell them when he had a mind to, but they wanted to see for themselves.

Obediah drove the wagon behind the pens where he kept the piney woods hogs. The wiry little creatures were only half tame. Like the swamp itself, these hogs did fine, wild or cultivated. But something had gotten them riled up today. They trotted around nervously inside the split rail fence.

As soon as they neared the pens, Edmond smelled something rank; a bear had been at the hogs again. The smell of bear was all over the place.

Edmond saw it first. He whistled his surprise and pointed out the spot to Ella. Just beyond the fence, at the edge of the open swampland lay an enormous heap of black fur matted with blood. A big black bear was lying dead outside the farthest hog pen! Splinters of pine stump were scattered over the carcass and the nearby ground. Edmond looked at Obediah. His overalls were torn and dirty. Had the bear attacked Pa?

Obediah leaned over the carcass and started to pull. Edmond and Ella scrambled to help. Pushing against the mound with their shoulders, they managed to get their arms underneath the huge creature. Then, half dragging, half shoving, they helped Pa load it onto the wagon.

Obediah nodded, and Edmond and Ella jumped onto the wagon boards. Then their pa winked at them and made a clicking noise with his tongue. The horses heaved into motion.

Edmond was sweating in the sticky heat. The smell of bear assaulted him. As they bumped along over the wiregrass, Ella gingerly lifted one of the bear's great paws. Long, thick claws curved over the heavy pads. A bit of cloth was caught under one of the claws. Edmond recognized the faded denim of Pa's overalls.

Ella said, "Where's Pa's rifle-gun at? Reckon he forgot it out by the pens?"

Edmond shrugged. Obediah Barber was not a man to be careless with his gun. Besides, Edmond didn't remember seeing Pa take the flintlock with him.

Ma came out of the kitchen as the wagon pulled into the yard. The youngest kids, Perry, Rosa, and baby Charles, trailed along beside her. Ma looked at the mound of bear on the back of the wagon. Then she looked closely at Obediah. "I'll send Lydia to get Matthew. He can help you skin it out."

Calmly, Ma went back to the kitchen to set out supper. Edmond and Ella followed Obediah to the water basin to wash. Edmond sure wished Pa would get talkative. There was a tale riding on the back of the wagon, and he couldn't wait to hear it!

Obediah did not say a word over supper. He finished eating before Matthew arrived. Edmond bolted down the rest of his meal so he could help the men. Skinning out a bear that size took a long time. It was hot, heavy work. The men didn't waste energy talking. It was well past dark when Pa, Matthew, and Edmond finished. The youngest children were already in their beds. The women were sitting on the porch, rocking.

Ella sat on the porch swing. She was stitching a new dress. Ella was big for eleven and already skilled in sewing. Ma and Lydia rested themselves. They had done most of the kitchen work. When the men came up to the porch, Lydia took a pitcher out to the well. She filled it with cool water and passed out glasses.

Everyone knew Pa couldn't be hurried. But nobody wanted to doze off and miss the first telling of the tale.

Finally, Obediah took a long drink. Then he settled back in his chair. He was in his storytelling position. Edmond perked up instantly. This was gonna be a whopper of a tale, for sure!

"That was some bear, Pa!" Edmond said. "You reckon they come any bigger?"

"I ain't never seen a bigger one," he said. "Never hope to, neither."

"How many bullets did you shoot before you killt it?" Ella asked.

Matthew said, "Come to think of it, Obediah, I didn't see any bullet holes in the hide."

Obediah chuckled. "That's 'cause there weren't none. The gun's hanging on the wall. I ain't touched it today." Obediah took a long sip. He was enjoying himself. Might as well let them drag the tale out of him!

"Did you trap the bear?" asked Ella. "Is that the varmint been eating the hogs?"

"I suspect that's the varmint all right," said Obediah. "But I didn't set no bear traps. Unless you count me as the bait."

Edmond's curiosity burst out, "Pa, did you kill it with your bare hands? How'd you do it?"

Obediah's eyes twinkled. He licked his lips, ready at last to tell the tale. "Well, I was down at the pens seeing 'bout the hogs. The rails had been knocked over again. 'Twas a wonder them hogs wasn't wanderin' all over creation!"

"Were you by yourself?" Ma asked.

"Nope, Nancy's husband was with me. I swannee, that Melton's a no-count scraper! I would've been better off by myself." Obediah had a disgusted look on his face.

Edmond was afraid Obediah would be out of chat again. His pa's mouth was tight shut, and his brow had gotten stormy. "Did the bear attack Melton, too?" Edmond asked.

"Naw, but I 'bout clobbered him, myself!" Obediah took a last gulp of his water and slammed the glass down on the arm of the rocker. He was silent for a minute. Then his face relaxed into a grin. "Aw, I guess I don't blame 'im. If I was as little as Melton is, I might've been afeard, too."

Obediah chuckled, as if he were watching the memory unfold. Then he continued. "We was heaving them rails back in place. All of a sudden, here comes such a calaberment from the hogs. You would've thought they were being tortured!

"Melton, he turns 'round to see what's going on. Then he goes to screaming: 'A bear! There's a bear!'

"So I turn 'round. I'm still holding the fence rail, mind ye." Obediah stood up to demonstrate. "Sure enough, there's this big black bear. One that size had to be a she-bear. She's raised up on her back legs, snarling. And she ain't ten feet away from us!"

Edmond grinned. He could imagine how it looked as he watched Pa act out the scene. Obediah Barber stood over six feet tall. And no more powerful man lived in the state of Georgia—not in 1881, nor any other time. Obediah was fifty-six years old and baby Charles was his fourteenth child. The man had already buried his first wife, Edmond's mother, in Kettle Creek Cemetery. But he was in the prime of life. One of the first of the swampers—a legend in his own lifetime!

"Well, I throwed that rail at the bear," Obediah said. "But the varmint ducked outta the way. Then she charged me. I thought I was a goner, for sure. I shouted for Melton to grab me one of them fat knots on the ground. Them pine stumps get hard as iron when they been laying around. But Melton, he was planted to the dirt. He couldn't have been less use if he was a tree. Made me so mad, he did! I just grabbed up the light'ood knot myself and took to crombing that bear.

"I thought I'd scare the varmint off. But she wouldn't scare. She was a' clawing and a' snarling, slinging her hot spit all over the place. I was beating her upside the head with the pinewood knot. Had to keep jumping outta the way of them big claws. I thought for sure the she-bear would give up and go back to the woods. But she kept at it. Right stubborn! And so I kept swinging at her. I'm pretty stubborn myself, you know!"

Edmond looked at the faces around the table. He thought he saw small smiles creeping across most every mouth. Obediah *was* a stubborn man! When he set out to accomplish something, nothing stood in his way. It took that kind of man to tame a wilderness like the Okefenokee.

"I landed one good, hard blow between the bear's eyes. I knew that one had done it when I heard the sound it made. Pieces of the light'ood knot went flying everywhere!

"That varmint wasn't plumb used up yet, though. She kept on clawing. But she wasn't moving right anymore. I reckon I knocked the sight out of her. I had to finish her off. I'd crushed her skull, and she was bound to die."

"Did Melton just stand there watching the whole time?" asked Matthew. "Or did he go for help?"

"I didn't pay no mind to Melton when the bear was after me. But once I knocked her down, I looked. And there he was, standing on that same clump of wiregrass! I was still holding what was left of the pine stump. Holding it in both my hands, like so." Obediah

held an imaginary club over his head with two hands. "I was all set to cromb that bear again if she started to raise up. I guess Melton thought I was fixing to cromb him, cause he like to have flew right off that spot when I gave him an eyeful!"

"Did the she-bear have cubs?" asked Matthew. "I never knowed a bear to let herself get killt in a fight, unless the dogs have backed her into a jam."

"I was thinking the same way," said Obediah. "So I went a little ways out on the prairie. And I seen 'em. Two cubs there was. But they was plenty big enough to strike out for theirselves. Them cubs ain't strong enough to come after the hogs yet. So I let 'em be. Maybe they'll take up in another part of the swamp before next summer."

The family sat quietly for a spell. Each person was digesting Obediah's tale. It was a whopper, all right! Edmond thought it was the best story he had ever heard! And he believed every word of it. Why, he'd seen the she-bear with his own eyes.

Matthew broke the silence. "I hear a black bear will only go for a penned hog when the berries are all gone. But once it gets a taste of hog, that bear never will leave the stock alone."

"That's what I know," agreed Obediah. "I trapped a bear a few weeks ago was messing with the hogs. When I lost that shoat last week, I kinda figured another bear had discovered the pens."

One part of the story bothered Edmond. Folks always said Obediah Barber wasn't afraid of anything. But Edmond knew his pa was a sensible man. Anybody who lives in the swamp learns a healthy respect for bear. "Why didn't you take the flintlock, Pa? If you knew there was a bear 'round the place...."

Obediah shook his head. "I didn't figure on the bear coming after me, son. Along and along, I've come upon a bear in the swamp. The bear always hightails it. Never knowed a varmint to come straight up to the pen and charge. Must've been heat-addled or something."

"I sure am glad you had Melton with you, Pa," said Ella.

"Did you sleep through the whole story, Ella?" Edmond threw up his hands. "Didn't you hear Pa? Melton was no more use than feathers on a gator. He jes' stood there and watched while the bear attacked." Edmond shook his head. What was the use in talking to a girl, anyway?

Ella fairly snarled at her brother. "I heard Pa, Edmond. All I meant was nobody would believe that story. But Melton was there. Melton saw it happen. And he ain't got nothing to boast about in that story, so folks will have to believe that Pa killt that bear." Ella looked at each of the listeners. "Don't you see? If it wasn't for Melton, folks would say the story was just the boasting of a Cracker!"

Edmond whooped. Some folks thought it was an insult to be called a Cracker. But the swampers were proud of the nickname. It was given to their Scotch-Irish ancestors by the British soldiers who thought the American farmers were noisy and boastful, "cracking" exaggerated tales. And Obediah Barber was a Cracker through and through! Everybody knew he was as proud of his tales as he was of his deeds. Some even said he got prouder every time his tales got better—and they got better with every telling!

Edmond hated to admit it, but his sister was right. If it wasn't for Melton, nobody would ever believe Pa's story.

"Ella's got a point, Pa," Edmond said. "Folks might've called the story a bald-faced lie. But Melton saw it happen. Now they'll have to believe Obediah Barber killt a bear with his own two hands. Someday they'll be calling you King of the Swamp!"

MORE ABOUT OBEDIAH AND THE SWAMP

Obediah Barber built his home at the edge of the Okefenokee Swamp. One of the earliest of the white settlers in this area, he was an accomplished outdoorsman. He was married three times and fathered twenty children. He died in 1909 at the age of eighty-four. The tale of Obediah and the bear is well known in Georgia's swamp country. Obediah's homestead has become a museum where his lifestyle and the famous incident are celebrated.

The Okefenokee swamp is the second largest freshwater swamp in the United States. Its Indian name, O-wa-qua-phenoga, meant "The Land of the Trembling Earth." Some of the words used in the story cannot be found in standard dictionaries. Expressions such as "cromb" (bang or hit), "calaberment" (commotion), and "light'ood knot" (pine stump) were part of the colorful language of the early swampers.

GEORGIA'S GHOST TOWN

Sarah and Synthia Stewart waved gaily to Mr. Tolbert in the post office as they skipped along the bank of Sweetwater Creek. Swinging the water bucket between them, they headed for the spring. The girls filled the water bucket and turned to go.

Synthia Stewart saw them first. She grabbed the arm of her older sister, Sarah, who was twelve. "Sarah, look over there!" Synthia pointed upstream.

Sarah looked over Synthia's shoulder. Both girls stood still. Fear and anger flashed in their eyes. They watched as the Federal soldiers set up their artillery in the distance.

Turning toward each other, the girls said at the same time, "Father would want...." Starting again, they said together, "Shouldn't we?" But before they could continue, Synthia turned, and her eyes were drawn to the windows of the factory. "They already know!" she whispered. The two girls gazed in silence at the mill workers peering from the upstairs windows.

The workers were watching the row of blue-uniformed soldiers as they made their way toward the factory. Synthia could see Martha Ann Tolbert watching from one of the windows. Martha Ann caught Synthia's eye. She waved frantically to the sisters to escape as quickly as possible.

The movement seemed to bring the girls out of their trance. Springing into action, they dropped their water bucket and ran back to the post office. The two girls burst through the door. Breathlessly they gasped that the hated Yankees were headed toward the factory.

Mr. Tolbert knocked an inkwell to the floor as he hurried around the counter of the post office and ran to the window. "They *are* here! We'd better warn the others," he muttered as he hurried next door to the community store, followed closely by Synthia and Sarah.

"Humphries!" Mr. Tolbert shouted. "The Feds are here, and they're headed straight for the factory!" He sank down on a stool and put his hands over his face. "My Martha! She's only sixteen! I knew we should've made her stay in school!"

In a few quick strides, Nathaniel Humphries made his way to the front of his store. He grabbed a box, went to the ammunitions shelf, and began to put bullets into the box. "Thomas," he said, "there's no time to spare! Help me get this stuff off the shelves. No sense in lettin' them help themselves to the ammo. They could turn around and use it on us!"

"We better go tell Ma and Grandma," Synthia said.

"They won't be surprised," Sarah said as they rushed out of the store.

"Why do you say that?" Synthia asked. "You mean because of the explosions yesterday?"

"Not entirely," Sarah replied. "You know Father used to be boss man at the mill. He always said the mill would be one of the targets if the North and South went to battle."

Synthia looked over her shoulder as she led the way up the hill toward the farm.

"Wish we didn't live so close to the factory!" Sarah observed, reading her sister's mind.

Synthia shivered at Sarah's comment. Even on this blazing July day, the woods seemed dark and ominous. Yesterday they'd heard explosions and seen blue clouds of smoke rising to the sky. The Confederates had burned the bridge across Sweetwater Creek to slow the Yankees' arrival. Today's silence had made it easy for Synthia to convince herself that the fighting had stopped. Either that or the Feds had moved in another direction. So much for wishful thinking!

"Where's the water?" Seven-year-old Jim looked puzzled as his sisters brushed past him. "Hey, what's wrong?" He hesitated. Then he followed them through the door of the log cabin.

Ma and Grandma stood motionless. Their eyes were riveted on Synthia and Sarah. Even four-year-old Isabella had stopped dressing her rag doll and was staring.

"Thank goodness you two are back," said Grandma. "When the neighbors told us what was going on, we were worried sick about you."

"I'm thirsty! What's wrong?" Jim was tired of always being the last to know.

His mother glanced at him briefly. "The Feds are marching on the factory. Your father and I had hoped it wouldn't come to this."

"Why the New Manchester Factory? What's so important about that?" Synthia knew her father had said it would be a likely target, but she did not understand why.

Mrs. Stewart had begun to pull silverware and dishes out of drawers and cabinets, so Grandma answered Synthia's question.

"Because the factory makes cloth for tents for our soldiers."

"But how did Pa know they'd find us?" Synthia persisted.

"It's because Pa knows everything," Jim said loftily. "He has to know. He's a sergeant in the Georgia Infantry."

"I just wish he hadn't been captured at Vicksburg," Synthia said.

"Well, at least we know he got away and is back with his regiment," Jim said.

"I hope he is safe, wherever he is fighting now," Sarah broke in, brushing away tears from her eyes.

"I just wish he were home," Ma said. "But we don't have time for wishing now. Sarah, you get that big water pitcher. Fill it full of all the silverware you can find. Synthia, you gather up the dishes and wrap them up in a linen cloth. We'll just see if they can find our things!"

The girls followed the directions as quickly as they could.

"Now, bring those things and follow me!" Ma led the way to a hollow stump a little way from the cabin. She lowered the water pitcher filled with silverware down into the hollow stump and placed the dishes around it. "Now, let's get all the limbs and brush we can find and make a pile over the stump. Won't look like nothin' important at all."

Martha Ann Tolbert was working at the spinning frame when she heard a shout she would never forget.

"Them cursed Yanks is comin' down Sweetwater Creek and headin' straight for us!"

Like every other worker in the factory, Martha Ann ran to the window. She stood on tiptoe and caught a glimpse of blue uniforms. For the hundredth time she wondered why she could not have been born taller. She dragged the platform the supervisor had built for her to the window. When she had started to work four years ago, she hadn't been able to reach the equipment. Here she was sixteen, and still needing the platform.

Martha Ann stood on her box and watched the scene unfolding in front of her. She glanced at the clock. It was ten o'clock in the morning on Saturday, July 2, 1864. She watched the fearsome line of blue-uniformed Yankees heading toward the factory. As surely as the millrace had changed the course of Sweetwater Creek, the war was changing forever the course of Martha Ann's life.

Martha Ann's attention was distracted by fellow mill workers as they joined her at the windows.

"Those crazy girls," Manning Gore muttered beside her.

Martha Ann followed Manning's gaze. She saw the Stewart girls as they stood gaping at the approaching cavalry. Would the soldiers capture the girls? With all her might, Martha Ann prayed the girls would look at her. She saw Synthia point to her.

Martha Ann motioned to the sisters to get out of the street. At her signal, the girls dropped the water bucket and ran toward the store. Martha Ann drew a deep sigh of relief. They would be safer there.

Martha Ann listened to the conversations around her.

"Looks like we'll be closin' up early," John Pitts observed.

"Guess Mrs. Stewart won't be comin' today to count and record what we got done," Manning Gore said.

"I always said it was our downfall fer sure to be makin' Confederate cloth for tents," James Stone said smugly.

"Wonder how Sherman found out about us," John Smith asked.

"Ol' Josiah knew what he was doin' when he took the currency out of the safe last week," Joseph Reeves commented. "How much was there?"

"Nearly a hundred thousand dollars, I heard tell," said James Stone.

"Lordy, they're gettin' close now! Wish we still had the Rebel Rangers," George Denney's voice quivered.

"That Company D was a good outfit, but their job was protectin' the cloth goin' on the wagons to Atlanta," Emanuel Hurt observed. "They weren't armed fer fightin' Union troops."

"Guess we all should've enlisted in the Georgia Infantry like Mr. Stewart did," Manning Gore added.

"Shouldn't we be doing something to get ready for their arrival?" Martha Ann asked.

"Too late now to do anything but pray." Manning touched Martha Ann's elbow.

Martha Ann could hear the Feds as they stormed the factory. Everyone froze as they heard the Union soldiers burst through the doorway downstairs.

"Who's in charge?" a harsh voice demanded.

Another Union soldier shouted, "Why, there's nobody but womenfolk and children here!"

"Not quite," said one of the workers. Martha Ann recognized the voice of Mr. Tippens.

"Who are you?" Union Major Haviland Tompkins inquired.

"A. C. Tippens. Head spinner and in charge of production," Mr. Tippens answered curtly. "You're makin' us lose precious work time."

Martha Ann caught the amused look of her friend John Pitts. Cicero Tippens was equal to any situation. He fixed the machinery at the mill, played the fiddle, and was especially good at resisting the efforts of the townspeople to reform his habit of using strong drink.

"And who are you?" thundered the Union officer.

"Henry Lovern, also in charge of production and overseer of the card room."

"You're both under arrest," pronounced the voice of the Union officer. "Along with every man, woman, and child in this factory. As long as no one tries anything foolish, you will be allowed to go westward to safety. Transportation will be arranged for you. One by one you will be escorted back to your homes. Henry Lovern, you are hereby instructed to permanently close down this mill."

Martha Ann looked at Manning Gore in dismay. With the rest of the factory workers on their floor, they gathered up their lunch pails and headed down the stairs.

Accompanied by Union soldiers, the factory workers walked out of the building and headed home. Martha Ann took a last look around the mill where she had spent a fourth of her life working as a machine operator. She had come to love the windows which were angled to allow in the most sunlight and the walls which were always freshly whitewashed. Since lanterns were not allowed because of the possibility of fire, the rooms were kept naturally bright. She saw several of her fellow workers and neighbors looking around as though bidding farewell to an old friend. The mill had provided them some income while so many of their menfolk were away fighting for the South. Now the fighting had come home.

The next morning Mrs. Stewart and Grandma were up early.

"The Yanks have taken over the town and closed down the factory," said Mrs. Stewart in a worried tone of voice. "It'll only be a matter of time before they find out I worked there as a record-keeper. I could tell them exactly how much we helped the Confederate government, right down to how many bundles of cloth were taken by our wagons to Marietta, and how many to Atlanta."

Synthia bolted out of bed as she heard her mother speak. She had not thought about her mother's involvement with the mill.

"Well, come what may," Grandma said. "Anyway, let's fix these children and our neighbors a meal to remember. We don't have much else, but we do have plenty of chickens. We might as well cook 'em all now so the Union soldiers can't go usin' our hens for target practice."

Synthia quickly got dressed. She had always loved to watch

Ma and Grandma get chickens ready for the frying pan. Usually they would fix three or four at a time, not the entire barnyard!

Ma and Grandma were quite a team! Ma grabbed the chickens and handed them to Grandma by the legs. Grandma took one chicken in each hand and gave them a quick twist, breaking their necks. The necks and heads went flying off in one direction. Then Grandma calmly tossed the bodies aside and took the next two Ma handed her. The whole process took only about ten minutes. Soon the whole front yard was littered with chickens without their heads. Each body was flopping wildly.

By now, Sarah, Jim, and Isabella had heard the commotion. They came running out of the cabin. With eyes as large as cannonballs, they stared at the headless chickens flailing about the yard.

As the chickens became still, the younger Stewarts brought them to Sarah and Synthia to be plucked. Ma gutted them and took them to Grandma who held them over the fire to singe any remaining feather hulls. After washing and cutting them up, Grandma put the chickens into the big iron frying pans. The smell of chickens frying permeated the cabin and yard.

After three hours of constant work, they all sat down at the table and bowed their heads. Grandma led the prayer.

"Gracious Father in heaven, we ask your blessing upon this family, and upon our Confederate soldiers as they fight for the Southern Cause. Keep special watch over our beloved Walter and keep us all safe in your loving care."

Synthia couldn't help but notice that the platter of chicken was already being passed before the final "amen."

The Stewart family then proceeded to enjoy the fine chicken dinner. They weren't finished when they heard the horses outside. The door of the cabin burst open and a voice growled, "Well, looks like we're just in time!"

Synthia looked out the open door. The entire yard was filled with Union soldiers. The officer who had entered signaled to the Stewart family to get up from their seats. He called the Union soldiers to come in and eat. Some trooped in and sat down. Others filled their plates and took them out to the porch. Synthia watched in disgust as they wolfed down the food.

Synthia and her family huddled together in the corner of the room. The soldiers generally behaved as though Synthia's family was not even there. Synthia could tell by her grandmother's expression it was all she could do to tolerate their behavior.

Synthia listened to their conversation. How strange they sounded with their rapid speech and clipped words!

"Sure tastes better than that foraged stuff what came from Mosley's place."

"I'll say! This is absolutely the best chicken I've ever eaten in my entire life."

"That's one thing these Rebs can do right!"

"Did they find anything when they searched the mill?"

"Just the company safe. It was empty."

"An empty safe, for a mill that produced up to 1200 yards of cloth a month! Do you believe that?"

"I guess not, what with a hundred and sixty-five people working there."

"Did you hear they burned the textile mills at Roswell? Three of them. One owner flew the French flag over the factory to fool our troops into thinking we better not burn it. Even deeded it to this French feller! Made Sherman madder than anything. Said it was a fictitious transfer and that such nonsense couldn't deceive him!"

"Where'd you hear this stuff?"

"Talked to some of Major Tompkin's men after they got back from Roswell. Somethin' big's gonna happen tomorrow, mark my words!"

Synthia didn't know when she fell asleep. She remembered sitting with her back to the wall and becoming very drowsy. At some point in the evening, she remembered a man's voice saying, "This youngun reminds me of my Joanie. Wish I could carry her to bed tonight." She felt herself being gently picked up and carried to her bed.

Synthia awakened the morning of July 9 to find Union soldiers "standing guard" in their cabin.

"Must be a rough assignment," Synthia thought scornfully. She hoped her father was in no more danger than the occupants of their cabin! She took the broom outside to sweep the porch. How Synthia wished she could sweep away the Union soldiers!

Suddenly Synthia heard a rushing and crackling sound. She looked down the hill and saw billows of smoke and orange flames lifting fiery fingers up the five floors of the mill. She dropped the broom and ran toward the fire. She caught snatches of conversation as she hurried along.

As she neared the mill, she joined a ring of onlookers. Martha

Ann was already there and came to stand beside her.

"Major Tompkins took eight men to the mill this morning," Martha Ann informed her. "They doused every floor with kerosene before they put the match to it. Word is, the community store's next."

Synthia watched in horrified fascination. The mill, one of the tallest buildings in the Atlanta area, stood engulfed in flames. All around her, people were crying.

The Union soldiers marched with their torches toward the community store. The townspeople followed them. Synthia watched the soldiers throw open the doors of the store.

One of the Union soldiers shouted, "You got fifteen minutes to take anything you want, then we burn it down."

Synthia hesitated. Did they really mean what they were saying, or was it some sort of a trick?

The officer looked at Synthia and asked, "You don't need anything?"

Synthia looked at Martha Ann. Then Synthia dashed in and grabbed a sack of flour. She noticed Martha Ann had a sack of sugar. The girls left quickly. A few minutes later, the store was ablaze.

That afternoon Federal officers ordered the townspeople to gather in one place. Synthia stood close to her mother. The officer began his announcement, but Synthia couldn't understand what he was saying. She waited until he was finished before asking her mother for an explanation.

"Well, Synthia," her mother began. "The townspeople were given two choices. We can either sign a paper saying we will no longer make cloth for the Confederacy, or we can be transported north of the Ohio River, where we won't be any help to the Southern cause." Synthia looked around to see what people were doing. Almost everyone chose to leave instead of signing the paper pledging allegiance to the Union.

The residents of New Manchester were allowed only a short time to gather a few possessions to carry with them. They were to travel by Federal wagons to Marietta, where they would board the train for the journey north.

From the last wagon, Synthia and Martha looked back toward the only hometown they had ever known. Today it was illuminated by fire. Tomorrow it would be a ghost town.

WHAT HAPPENED AFTER THE FIRE

Most of the New Manchester residents were never heard from again. Martha Ann Tolbert lived in Ohio until after the war. She then returned to the New Manchester area and married Yancy Boynton. Their house in Powder Springs is still standing.

Synthia Stewart and her family were sent to Louisville, Kentucky. Synthia's sister Sarah died at the age of thirteen, one year after the move. The rest of the Stewarts were reunited with Synthia's father after the war. They returned to New Manchester and found everything in ruins and overgrown. Much to their surprise, they found the silverware and china in the hollow stump where they had hidden it. In the ashes of their homestead, thousands of strawberry plants were growing. The Stewart family gathered the fruit and sold it in Atlanta to make a living that year. That was the only year the fields produced strawberries in New Manchester!

THE SECRET SCHOOL

"Miz Beasley! Miz Beasley!" Lily shouted as she burst through the door.

The children gasped. Nobody entered Mrs. Beasley's classroom shouting! All of the small, brown faces turned to see how their teacher would react.

"Miz Beasley," Lily panted. She was breathless from running. "The patty-rollers got George!"

The children froze. Lily's brother had been caught! What would they do to him? Would he be whipped? Taken away from his parents? Would the rest of Mrs. Beasley's students be found out? In the children's minds, questions fluttered like moths seared by a flame.

Mathilda Beasley rose slowly. To her students, she was as tall as a mountain and just as majestic. Calmly, she walked over to Lily.

Lily stood by the door. Her hands trembled. Tears collected on the rims of her eyes. Mrs. Beasley put a gentle hand on the girl's shoulder. "Is George on the square, Lily?"

Lily nodded, pointing out the direction.

Mrs. Beasley looked at the children. "Put away your books,

boys and girls. It's time to work on your mending. I'll return as soon as I can." She reached for her shawl and slipped out the door.

The children were too frightened to talk. They quickly gathered all the books and stacked them in a bin beneath the window seat. Suddenly, their precious books felt like red-hot coals. These books could burn the fingers that touched them!

The children sat on their benches. They darned socks. They mended sleeves. They jumped each time a needle struck a thimble. Mrs. Beasley often comforted them by reading from the Bible. But the children knew it would be dangerous to open a book today. At any moment, the patty-rollers might throw open the door. It was illegal to teach reading or writing to black children in Savannah in 1859. The children were breaking the law simply by coming to Mrs. Beasley's school!

Mathilda walked briskly in the direction Lily had pointed out. She thought she knew where George had been caught. A group of white youths had been hanging around Johnson Square, looking for someone to harass. The patty-rollers, as they were called in the black community, were white males assigned to patrol duty. Their job was to enforce the laws concerning Negroes, like the night curfew that had been enacted to keep black people from meeting to plot against slave owners.

Mathilda checked to be sure she had her pass. By day, all blacks had to show their passes to the patrolmen. Without a pass, it was illegal for a black person to do business in the city. Even free blacks had to carry passes signed by their white guardians. Mathilda was a free woman of mixed ancestry. Her father was a Native American and her mother was Creole, of French and African blood. To the patty-rollers, though, Mathilda was simply a Negro. She had to carry a pass that allowed her to take in sewing and buy supplies for her husband's restaurant.

The hubbub reached Mathilda's ears before she spotted George. The little boy was in the center of a small crowd. Three white males surrounded him. One held George by his collar. Another was gesturing with a book. "Look, boy, who does this book belong to? Where'd you get it?"

George's eyes were glued to the face of his questioner. He was too terrified to speak. And he couldn't shake his head because his collar was held fast against his jaw.

Mathilda took a deep breath. Her mind raced. How could she get George away safely? She had to be careful. The patrol could turn on her. According to Savannah laws, the punishment for a free black caught teaching blacks to read was a fine of one hundred dollars. That was a small fortune! In addition to the fine, there was a penalty of thirty-nine lashes. The law was often ignored both by blacks and by whites who sympathized with the slaves. But these patty-rollers would not be sympathetic. They were making a show of capturing George. Mathilda knew they would enjoy adding a black woman to the nasty display.

The patty-rollers were in no hurry. They swaggered in front of the crowd. Why, the three were mere boys themselves! Mathilda would bet that not a one had seen his seventeenth birthday. Think of them having the right to bully a little fellow! And only because

he wanted to learn to read and write. Mathilda wondered if any of the patrolmen could read—or even had the desire to learn.

She stepped through the crowd. An uncommonly tall woman, Mathilda towered over the patty-rollers. She spoke with a clear, rich voice in flawless English. "Why are you holding this child?"

The patrol turned on her. Great tears began to roll down George's cheeks at the sight of his teacher. "This your boy?" one of the youths asked in a rough voice.

"George is not my son," Mathilda replied calmly.

"Then mind your own business, aunty," the youth grumbled.

"George *is* my business," Mathilda said firmly. "I am his teacher."

The small crowd seemed to catch its breath. Was Mrs. Beasley confessing that she taught black children to read and write? Everybody knew the penalty for breaking the law. George began to whimper.

"George comes to my house each day for instruction on mending and the proper care of linens." Mathilda smiled politely. "He's a very promising student."

"Since when do boys learn to do washin' with a book?" the patty-roller sneered at Mathilda. "Last I heard, they use soap to do washin'!"

Mathilda prayed her voice would remain steady. It pained her to lie. She was a devout Catholic, and she lived by her religious principles. But she had a classroom full of innocent children to protect. It was not a sin to be born with brown skin. Nor was it a sin to cultivate the mind. In fact, it was a sacred duty. Little George had done nothing wrong. And neither had Mathilda Beasley!

"George was bringing the book so I could show him how to make a sack to keep it in." Mathilda looked steadily at the white youth. Neither her voice nor her face showed any hesitation. "Books are costly. They last much longer if they are carried inside a cloth pouch. Making a cloth pouch is an excellent project for a student."

The bully did not appreciate the lesson on how to care for books. He shook the book at Mathilda. "How come this black boy has a book to make a pouch for? Huh? It's against the law to sell a book to a black person."

Mathilda looked into the youth's eyes. "The book does not belong to George." At least this was the truth, she thought.

"Then who did he get it from?" asked the patty-roller.

"He got the book from me," Mathilda said simply. Again, the crowd seemed to hold its breath. "Many of my husband's business associates have libraries." This was also true. Many of the men that Abraham did business with were wealthy enough to own fine libraries. Of course, Abraham and Mathilda had a library of their own. And this book had come right out of the Beasley home.

"You just full of answers, ain't you, aunty?" taunted one of the white youths.

Another member of the patrol took up the complaint: "So this here George is a 'promising student,' huh? How come you let him run around with a book? Ain't you never heard of the law in this state? It's illegal for a black person to have a book. Everybody knows he ain't smart enough to do any book-learning. A body just might make a mistake and whup this here 'promising student' of yours. Sure does look like he's been taking what don't belong to him!"

Mathilda spoke with authority. "George learns responsibility when he carries this book to school each day. I would assume that the people of Georgia want black boys to be trustworthy and responsible."

The white youth shrugged. He was awfully tired of this conversation. All these folks were crowded around listening. And this black woman talked so fancy—she sounded like a lawyer from Boston! "Well, just you take your 'promising student,' then." He shoved George at Mathilda. "Maybe you better learn him how to walk, so this 'promising student' don't go dropping his sewing project all over the street."

The other patty-rollers threw George's book and pile of linens on the ground. One of them spit on the things. Then the three ran off.

Mathilda calmly knelt in front of George. She wiped his tears with her handkerchief. She laid her hands on his shoulders. The little boy's body shuddered as he made a great effort to stop crying. Mathilda looked deep into his brown eyes. Then she grinned and winked. That did it! George jumped on her. He threw his arms around her and gave her a big hug.

The crowd chuckled. Somebody picked up the pile of linens from the ground and shook off the dirt. Somebody else retrieved the book. Mathilda wrapped the book in the linens and handed the bundle to George. He took the load carefully, making sure the book could not be seen under the linens. This was the way Mrs. Beasley's students came to school each day. They walked to her house alone, carrying their schoolbooks inside a pile of clothes to be mended.

Mathilda looked at George with pride. He was one of her

youngest students. His parents worked hard to send him and Lily to school. It was rare for a black family to be able to send two children to school. She gave a silent prayer of thanks that George had been delivered from the patrol. Mathilda refused to let her mind dwell on all the things that could have happened to George, to her other students, or to herself. She took George's hand, thanked the folks for picking up George's things, and walked back to school. As always, she walked with her head high.

Lily stabbed her finger with the needle when she heard the footsteps. She stuck her wounded finger in her mouth and turned to face the door. When she saw George, she sprang off the bench and hugged him. He was the best little brother in the world! She wondered why she hadn't realized that before today!

The other students had dozens of questions.

"Did they whup you?"

"What happened?"

"How'd they know you were carrying a book?"

George didn't know which question to answer first. He giggled. "Naw, they didn't whup me. But they was gonna. Miz Beasley took up for me, and they let me go. Don't nobody talk better'n Miz Beasley!"

Mrs. Beasley hung her shawl on the hook. She let the children chatter for a while. Then she walked to the front of the room. "Lily, did you see what happened? George says he fell, and his book came tumbling out. He says the patrol grabbed him before he had time to stand up."

"Yes, Miz Beasley," Lily said. "I saw the whole thing. George was walkin', lookin' straight ahead. Jes' like you taught us. One of them patty-rollers stuck out his boot. That's why George fell. The patty-rollers tripped him."

Mathilda's eyes filled with tears as she listened. She told the children to bow their heads in prayer.

"Miz Beasley, what should we pray?" asked Lily.

"Let us thank the Lord for delivering George. And for giving him courage in his ordeal." Mathilda smiled at George.

"Miz Beasley," asked George. "Should we pray for the patty-rollers, too?"

Mathilda was quiet for a long moment. "Yes, George," she said at last. "Let us pray for the patty-rollers' feet."

"For their feet, Miz Beasley?" asked Lily.

"Yes, for their feet." Mathilda's eyes were sparkling. "Let us pray that God gives the patty-rollers large feet. So we can see them when they try to trip us!"

MORE ABOUT THE AMAZING MATHILDA

Mathilda Beasley was a remarkable woman. Born Mathilda Taylor in New Orleans in 1834, she was orphaned as a young girl. She came to Savannah and married Abraham Beasley, a wealthy black widower. Mathilda ran a secret school for black children before the Civil War.

After Abraham died, Mathilda became a Catholic nun—the first black nun in Georgia—and gave her estate to the Catholic church. Fondly called Mother Beasley, Mathilda established an orphanage for black girls in Savannah and helped to run it until her death in 1903. Eighty years later, the city of Savannah established a park across from the site of the orphanage and named it in her honor.

AURARIA'S NUGGET

William Green Russell woke with a start. At first he could see nothing in the inky darkness. He lay stiffly silent. He stole a glance at Levi, who was sleeping soundly on his side of the bed. Surely Levi's gentle breathing wouldn't have awakened him so suddenly.

Then Green felt it. Something was moving across his chest! A light but distinct weight was making steady progress toward his left arm. He came tearing up out of the bed. The quilts and comforter tangled around his legs and slowed his progress. A strangled yell escaped from his lips.

"What's wrong?" Levi sat halfway up in bed. "Why're you yellin'?" He fumbled around for the candle and finally got it lit.

Green was standing in the corner. He could barely make out the shape of his brother stumbling across the room. His eyes looked like two pieces of coal shining in the candlelight. "Something was in bed with us!" His voice was somewhere between a scream and a stammer.

On the other bed, little Oliver sighed deeply and rolled over.

"I must've hit you when I turned over," Levi said. "Bring the covers back, Green!" Levi whined and rolled into a ball. "I'm catchin' my death while you're standin' over there gapin'?"

Glancing warily around in the flickering candlelight, Green headed back toward the bed. Hastily, he tossed the covers back onto the mattress, then dived under the quilts.

Green lay awake for a long time, listening to the wind howling through the trees. He watched the white curtains at the windows swell and sink with each gust of wind. Like many of the buildings built during the Gold Rush, the Russell cabin had been built in a hurry. Probably a good thing they didn't try to heat the boys' room. All the heat would escape through those loose-fitting windows.

Finally the sky started to lighten with the first gray hint of morning. Only then did Green drift off into a fitful sleep. When he awakened, the room was bright. He dressed quickly in the cold bedroom. He could hear voices from the kitchen.

"Quite a wind we've got out there," Grandpa Russell said as the door banged shut. "Green up yet?"

Green knew Grandma was frying bacon. The warm smell floated down the hallway and crept into the bedroom, inviting him to hurry. He splashed his face and washed his hands with the frigid water in his washbowl. Ice crystals had formed around the inside curve of the bowl, making a perfect circle where they floated on the water's surface.

Green heard Levi's voice. "Green had a nightmare last night. Prob'ly didn't sleep too good. He 'bout scared me to death." After a pause he added, "Sure was diff'rent. Usually little Oliver's the one that's thrashing around. Green sleeps as soundly as the dead folks out in Auraria Cemetery!" Levi paused, then asked, "Where's Pa?"

"Your pa left early this morning. He went up to Dahlonega." Green heard the clatter as Grandpa Russell stacked more wood in the stove. "You know Auraria should'a been the county seat, don't you? The land Auraria is settin' on went to the wrong person in the land lottery. This fella didn't even have clear title!" He closed the stove door with a bang and adjusted the squeaky vent. "I swear, there were more lawyers 'round here than fools got pyrite. Kept right busy too, what with folks claimin' to own the same land."

Green dressed quickly and slipped quietly into the kitchen. It seemed to him that everyone's morning greeting was heartier than usual. His brothers had probably talked about his nightmare. He could still feel that slow steady weight as it moved across his chest. He shuddered.

As he pulled his chair up to the table, Grandma Russell passed him a plate loaded with bacon and scrambled eggs. Green shook his head.

"Ain't you gonna eat, boy?" Grandpa asked.

The bacon smelled so good. But Green really did not feel like eating. "I'm not very hungry, Grandpa," he responded.

"You ain't sick, are ya?" Grandpa reached over and touched Green's arm.

Green shook his head and took a small bite of the bacon.

Grandpa Russell kept talking. "You know, nice pork like this used to sell for two and a half cents a pound back when Auraria was a boom town. But not in '34. Couldn't find a pound of bacon to buy anywhere that summer!"

Grandpa Russell took another helping of eggs before he continued. "Good market for pork here 'bouts. Them miners, they weren't about to stop diggin' for gold and go shootin' fer somethin' to eat. So, we got hog drives from Tennessee, sometimes from Kentucky. Them drovers took the low country—valleys and gorges through the mountains. Easier travelin'." He glanced at Green. "You ever seen the old slaughter pen at the edge of town?"

Green nodded.

"That's where they kept them hogs when they got here. Some of the housewives here 'bouts got mighty good at slaughtering." Grandpa Russell winked at Grandma.

"They did?" Green asked.

"Sure we did, Green. The miners paid in gold nuggets. We liked that gold as well as the next person!" Grandma Russell said. "Kept our knives sharpened all the time. We wanted to be ready when the drovers came."

"That was no easy job, bein' a drover. Them hogs was stubborn. They generally went in the opposite direction they were prodded." Grandpa Russell chuckled. "They had turkey drives, too. Bein' a turkey drover was even worse! Come evenin', the turkeys took to the trees to roost. Couldn't get 'em down till mornin'. Then the dang birds would fly away in every direction."

Green grinned.

"Probably some of them turkeys is still out there in the woods. Or maybe some of their great, great grandturkeys!"

Try as he might, Green could not relax. His mind kept returning to that strange sensation of something moving across his chest.

On their way to school, Levi and Oliver seemed to sense

Green's somber mood. Instead of starting the day with a snowball fight, they decided to go on inside. The boys burst through the door of the one-room schoolhouse. A gust of cold air entered with them.

"Hello, boys." Miss Smithson was sweeping the floor. "You're here just in time. It's finally starting to get warm in here."

The brothers could feel the fingers of heat reaching out toward them from the potbellied stove. Levi threw his coat toward the hook. He craned his neck toward the group of children in the back of the room. They had started a game of marbles.

"Hey, Green. Did ya bring your new cats-eye shooter?" asked Frank. "You ready to trade yet? This one ain't treatin' me right."

There was a roar of laughter from the circle of children. The marble had ricocheted off the leg of the bench and hit Lucky, the school cat, on the head. She opened her gold eyes disdainfully and stretched. She arched her back, pushing her twelve toenails out of the twelve toes of her front feet.

"Frank, maybe you need an extra finger on each hand like Lucky. Cats with extra toes are always good luck. Maybe it would work for you, too."

"I like fishin' better than shootin' marbles anyway." Frank put his shooter in his pocket. "Don't need special stuff to use, neither." He glared at the children who were taking their seats. "Lot quieter, too!"

"You're right," said Green. "Remember when we couldn't find anything to use for sinkers on our fishing lines?"

"Yeah, we went up to the Signet's old printing office and

found some rusty lead type. That worked real good," said Frank.

"I've still got mine," Green said.

"Don't need to keep it. You can still find some on the ground over there," said Frank.

After school Green and his brothers walked back the mile and a half to the Russells' house in town.

"Did you hear Grandpa this morning? He said that when Auraria was only ten months old, there were eighteen to twenty stores and 1,000 people here!" said Oliver. He jumped over a rock which was half-covered with snow. "Can you believe that? Aren't near that many folks here now."

"Well, the gold was lots easier to find back then," Green pointed out. "Didn't have to dig so much for it. Some miners just picked it up. Stories like that brought all kinds of people. You know what Auraria means, don't you?" He glanced at Oliver. "Gold mine—that's what it means."

"Really?" Oliver's eyes sparkled.

"Wasn't the town first named Nuckollsville after that fella who built the hotel?" asked Levi.

"Yep, Nathaniel Nuckolls built the hotel. It was the second building in town. Overrun with guests, too. Folks couldn't wait to get their hands on some of that gold." Green poked Levi and motioned for him to look at Oliver. Oliver had lifted several rocks to look under them.

"No gold there," Oliver announced.

As they drew closer to the Russells' house, Green noticed that the smoke from the chimney was curling into an unusual shape.

"Levi, look at that! Doesn't it look just like a question mark?" Green pointed to the smoke above the chimney. "I think we live in a mystery house, and it's trying to tell us something!"

When Green got to bed that night, he couldn't sleep. He lay awake long after Levi and Oliver's breathing became deep and regular.

Suddenly Green heard a soft rustle and a "meow" over by the window. He slowly sat up in bed. On the floor sat a yellow cat with glowing gold eyes. Green reached out his hand toward the cat. It sauntered toward him and leaped nimbly onto his bed.

"So it was *you* last night!" thought Green. The cat purred as he stroked its back. He noticed a faint ammonia smell coming from the cat. It smelled like it had just walked across a freshly-mopped floor. "What's your name?" The cat shook its head like it didn't want to say. Green picked up a front paw. "Hey, you've got six toes on your front paws, just like Lucky! Is your name Lucky, too?"

The cat jumped down from the bed and scampered across the floor. Waiting for the moment when the curtains billowed out, it leaped to the windowsill. Green admired the cat's timing as he fell back onto his pillow.

When Green awakened, he headed straight for the window. The cat was gone. He looked under the beds and in the closet. The bedroom door was closed and his brothers were still asleep. He walked to the window and looked out across the yard. No cat in sight. As he stood at the window, his gaze centered on the latch. The window was securely locked! Perhaps Levi got up in the night to go to the outhouse. Maybe the cat slipped out then.

Green quickly got dressed as Levi started to stir. "Levi," he asked, "did you go outside during the night?"

"No," he said between yawns. "Why?"

"I can't figure out where the cat came from," Green said.

"What cat?" Levi asked.

"Grandma Russell's new cat, I guess." Green could still almost feel those feet moving across his chest. "It was in our room again last night."

Oliver sat straight up in bed. "Where's a cat?" He looked under his bed.

"What are you talkin' about? You know Grandma Russell doesn't like cats," Levi said. "You must've been dreamin' again."

"I'm tellin' you it was not a dream! I petted it. I heard it purr and meow. It even had six toes, like Lucky. It smelled kinda bad, too, like ammonia. It got up in bed with me again," Green said.

"What do you mean, *again?*" Levi said.

"That's what happened the night before! It had to be! It felt exactly like a cat walking across my chest," Green said. "I can't understand why you don't believe me!"

"No," Grandma Russell said when the boys came in. "I don't have a new cat. Why do you ask?"

Grandpa and Grandma Russell listened intently. Grandpa Russell scratched his head thoughtfully. "There's something about your story that reminds me...If'n I could jes' remember..."

"What did this cat look like?" Grandma Russell asked.

"It was a large yellow cat with tiger stripes and big gold eyes," Green began. "Had six toes on its paws and smelled like ammonia."

"Nugget!" Grandpa Russell jumped up from the table and started opening drawers in the buffet.

"Mercy, Robert, what are you looking for?" Grandma Russell asked.

"The article. Don't you remember? About when the Fire King came to town. Back durin' the Gold Rush? Called himself the Cat Man. Remember? He used ammonia!" Grandpa Russell was still pulling drawers out and in like a shadowboxer.

"Here, let me find it." Grandma Russell pushed back her chair. "The way you're going at it, I won't have one linen tablecloth fit to use come Sunday!"

Grandpa Russell sat down obediently.

"Who was the Fire King, Grandpa Russell?" Green asked.

"Well, he came to Auraria to entertain folks, November of 1833. Knew the miners had lots of gold and nowhere to spend it. He put that announcement in the *Western Herald* about his show so everybody'd come. And everyone did," Grandpa Russell said.

"Here," Grandma Russell said, pulling a yellowed newspaper from the bottom drawer. Green could read the headlines from where he sat: "FIRE! FIRE! FIRE!"

"That's the way he started his show—by eatin' fire. He even taught five or six folks from here how to do it. They were overnight wonders! Great show—saw it myself." Grandpa Russell's eyes had a faraway look.

"Did you say he had a cat?" Oliver asked.

"No, he didn't bring a cat with him. He used one of the Auraria cats," Grandpa Russell said. "Fact is, the one he used looked like the cat Green jes' described. Funny cat. Everyone called it Nugget. Used to go with the miners every day down into the mines. Kinda got to be a good luck charm to them."

"Why?" Green asked.

"Sorta had the idea it'd keep 'em safe. You know, air must be all right if the cat was still there," Grandpa Russell said.

"Why did the cat man want a cat?" Oliver asked.

"For his famous 'Cat O' Nine Lives' trick. He would put a cat to death by makin' it smell prussic acid. Then he'd bring it back to life by havin' it smell ammonia. Well, he put Nugget to death all right. Then, after he brought it back, it had some kind of fit," Grandpa Russell said.

"Didn't he complain about the ammonia here being too weak?" Grandma Russell asked.

"Yep," answered her husband. "So somebody went out and got him some stronger ammonia."

"Always appeared to me like the prussic acid must've been too strong rather than the ammonia too weak," Grandma Russell observed.

"Did he ever get Nugget to come back to life?" Oliver asked eagerly.

"He did get the cat to come around, but it took a long time. Then he got the idea of putting it in the open air away from the crowd to hurry its recovery," Grandpa Russell said.

"As I recall, that wasn't too good an idea," Grandma Russell said.

"Nope, when they brought that cat in a little while later, it was dead." Grandpa Russell said. "Cold, stiff, and dead!"

Levi shuddered. "What a horrible story!"

"Wait! That's not the end," Grandpa Russell said. "Fact is, the next mornin' a bunch of the men were sittin' around the *Western Herald* office. And what comes boundin' into the room? This same yeller cat, Nugget! Newspaper editor was there, and he seen it. So did the miners that was there. They all swore it was the same identical cat! One of the miners even said it was in pretty good spirits, considering.'"

"That's a terrific story, Grandpa Russell," Green exclaimed. "Did anyone ever see the cat after that?"

"Yep, sure did!" Grandpa Russell said. "And this is where you come into the story."

"Me?" asked Green.

"Yes, you," said Grandpa Russell. "You're gonna be havin' some incredible good luck."

"Why do you say that?" Green asked.

"I'm not jes' sayin' it—it's a fact for sure!" Grandpa Russell pushed his chair back from the table. He took out his pipe and pushed the cold tobacco down with his finger. "Nugget hasn't been seen in these here parts for years now. Guess maybe we all thought he'd done used up all his nine lives, at least until last night."

"Have other people seen Nugget, I mean since the newspaper office?" asked Green.

"You bet! Colonel Gibson said he saw the cat just the day before he found that chunk weighing nine pounds and three ounces." Grandpa Russell took a long pull at his pipe. "That chunk had lots of gold in it, too. Colonel Gibson counted 124 particles of gold on the surface. Took it from the bed of the Chestatee River. I read about that find in the newspaper myself."

"Didn't Alfred Holt make a big find too? And he laid credit for his fortune to the cat?" Grandma Russell asked.

"By gum, that's right!" Grandpa Russell took his pipe out of his mouth and leaned forward. "He found a big rock weighing over twenty pounds. It had pieces of gold in it the size of marbles!"

"And then there was Major Hockenhull over at the Battle Branch. He made a heap o' money." Grandpa Russell chuckled. "Now he says seein' that cat had absolutely nothin' to do with it! But there's folks here who'll tell you different!"

"Sounds like McLaughlin," Grandma Russell said.

"Yep, him too," Grandpa Russell snorted. "Found him a specimen from his mine that was four-fifths gold. But not until he'd caught sight of Nugget. The *Western Herald* had an article about his find, too."

"Green, why didn't you wake me up?" Levi demanded.

"Me, too!" said Oliver. "I want to see this cat!"

"I know men in these here parts that would cut off their right arms for a look at that cat," Grandpa Russell said. "Fact is, wish you'd come and got me! It can't have too many of them nine lives left. Sure would like to see that critter 'fore it runs slap out!"

"Do you promise me you'll wake me up if he comes back?" Oliver pleaded.

"I promise. I'll wake everybody up. Then we can all get rich together!" Green said happily.

GETTING RICH ON GOLD!

Green, Levi, and Oliver Russell left Georgia in February of 1858. They discovered gold in the region that is now Colorado. They named their new settlement Auraria in honor of their hometown in Georgia. Stories of their gold finds started the famous Pike's Peak Gold Rush of 1859. In April, 1860, the settlement was renamed Denver.

When gold was discovered in 1829 in north Georgia, ten thousand hopeful prospectors became part of the nation's first gold rush. A mint was built in Dahlonega (the name means "yellow metal") and about six million dollars worth of gold coins were eventually minted there.

CHEROKEE TEARS

Spring, 1835, Head of the Coosa River, northwest Georgia

"Hey, git out of here!" shouted the red-bearded man as he rode into the yard in front of the Ross home.

Five-year-old G. W. dropped the kernels of corn he was holding out for his pet peacock, Chief. The startled bird lowered his huge fan-shaped tail and skittered toward the trees, stirring up a trail of dust with his tail feathers. G. W. stared at the man who had just ordered him out of his own yard.

The stranger jumped from his horse, tying the reins to the railing on the front porch of G. W.'s home. He rubbed his hands together eagerly as he stared at the two-story house with all the brick chimneys and the twenty glass windows. He turned his gaze once more to where G. W. sat frozen to the ground. The man's eyes narrowed. "You still here?" he snarled. "Go on. I said git out of here!"

His eyes wide with fright, G. W. leaped to his feet. Running almost before he was standing, he tripped and went sprawling on the ground.

The red-bearded man laughed heartily.

Tears streamed down G. W.'s burning face as he picked himself up and ran stiffly through the front door. "Ma! James! Allen! Silas! There's a man out there who says we have to get out," he wailed.

James opened the door of the house and stepped out onto the porch. Allen was right behind him. "What did you say to our little brother?" James asked.

"Name's Hugh Brown. Where's John Ross? This is his place, ain't it?" the bearded man demanded.

"Our father is in Washington, D.C., right now. He'll be home soon," James answered.

"Soon ain't soon enough! This is my place now," the stranger shouted.

"We built this home ourselves," James began.

"It's *my* place now." The man rushed James with a flood of words. "Won it in the land lottery day before yesterday. I'm having a look around to see what all I've won. Then I'm going to get my family. We'll all be moving here in three, maybe four days. And that means you'll have to go somewheres else." The man started for the front door.

James and Allen stood close together, blocking the door to the house. "What proof do you have that you've won our home?"

The man fished in the pocket of his homespun shirt and brought out a piece of paper. "See here. Says Land Lot 237, 23rd District, 3rd Section." He showed them the corresponding map. The Ross land lay where the Etowah and Oostanaula Rivers met and formed the Coosa River.

This time the man walked around the side of the house into

the backyard. The Ross brothers followed. The man squinted at the scene before him. "This is some place you've got here—outbuildings, animals, the Coosa River, even a peacock!" He chuckled at his good fortune. He wheeled and headed for the door to enter the large two-story house. "Now let's take a look inside," he said to the two brothers.

"Our ma's in there, and she's sick," James protested. "We don't have anyplace to go. At least let us stay here until our father returns."

"Your pa's the chief of the Cherokee Nation, that right?"

James and Allen looked at each other and then nodded.

The man looked across the well-kept fields and was silent for several moments. "Well, reckon there's enough room for all of us for a time. But not in the main house. You folks can stay in those buildings out back." Abruptly, he mounted his horse and rode away.

James and Allen Ross watched the man ride off through the trees. He finally disappeared into the distance, leaving behind a trail of dust and a sense of dread that would not go away.

G. W. had crawled up on the bed right next to Ma. They stopped talking and looked up hopefully as James and Allen entered the house. Their mother, Quatie, was very weak from her illness. Her face was as pale as her bedding.

"Did you make that bad man leave?" G. W. asked. "He scared me."

"He left, but he said he'd be back soon to claim our land," Allen said.

"I don't think I have the strength to go anywhere," Ma murmured.

"We won't have to leave today," James answered. "Not until Pa gets back."

"I'm not going to leave!" G. W. announced hotly. "They can't make me, and I won't go!"

"Let's wait and see what Pa has to say when he returns from Washington City," Ma said weakly. "Maybe he persuaded the federal government to help us. And even if we do have to leave, maybe it won't be for too long."

"Why did Pa leave us here if someone could come and take our home away?" G. W. asked. "Isn't he worried about us?"

"Of course Pa is worried about us, but he is trying to help *all* the Cherokee people," Ma said. "You know how well educated Pa is and how well he speaks. He is the best one to argue for our rights. And, he is the Principal Chief." She sighed and turned to her older sons. "We'll need baskets to pack our things in. James, you and Allen will have to strip more bark from the white oak trees so I can weave some more."

"I can help, too," said G. W.

"Sure, you and Silas can help," James said. He looked worriedly at Ma. "I'm sure this is all a mistake. When Pa returns, he'll straighten it out." He motioned to everyone to leave. Ma had already closed her eyes.

The Ross sons gathered bark and made strips for their mother to weave into baskets. Usually Quatie made beautiful colors from the poison ivy root and skillfully wove intricate designs into graceful shapes. But now there was no time for all that. She worked quickly to fashion large rough baskets to use in their journey away from the home they loved.

When the Brown family arrived a week later to claim their

new home, the Ross sons did their best to make their mother comfortable in the storage room out back. Worried about their mother's health, the family anxiously awaited their father's return.

Five-year-old G. W. was the first to hear John Ross's horse. "Pa, Pa! We're back here. Make those people get out of our house! They even think my peacock is theirs!" Big tears welled up in G. W.'s eyes. "I want Chief back!"

John Ross knelt to hug little G. W. "I know all about it. Hugh Brown met me at the gate and grabbed the reins of my horse! Says he now owns everything here!" He gave G. W. another hug. "But he doesn't own you or your brothers. Let's go inside and see Ma."

John Ross squinted as his eyes became adjusted to the dim light in the outbuilding where his family was living. Tears came to his eyes. "I have been trying to help the Cherokee people, but I cannot even help my own family," he murmured to himself.

Quatie was very weak, but John could see she had been trying to weave baskets. He put his hand on her forehead. She smiled up at him weakly. "Were you successful in Washington City?"

John shook his head wearily.

"John, how can the state of Georgia give away our land and possessions? We *own* this place," Quatie said.

John looked at his Cherokee wife. "The state of Georgia says the Cherokee cannot own property in Georgia. So they say this property is not ours." He took Quatie's hand in his.

"Does everyone in the whole state want us to leave?" G.W. asked anxiously.

"No, not everyone," John Ross smiled at his young son. "Many of our neighbors are our friends."

"Why don't we fight to get our home back?" G. W. reached for a piece of flint he had shaped into a sharp point for his spear.

"First," his father answered, "Because they have the Georgia law on their side, and second, because we are greatly outnumbered and we could cause even more misfortune to befall our people. But, most of all, because fighting is not the right way to change people's minds," John Ross spoke gently. "There must be a better way. I want to show the lawmakers in Washington City what is happening and tell them what is best for the Cherokee people. We have lost too much land already. We cannot keep giving it up. And we should not have to. The lawmakers must see that the government needs to help us!" John's face had reddened and a vein bulged in his left temple.

"But why our place?" G. W. persisted. "There's lots of land in Georgia. Why do they want ours?"

"Some people are greedy," John Ross answered. "And when they see what the Cherokee have, they see land already cleared, ready for farming. They see that some of us have homes better than their own. But, above all, they think about the gold that has been discovered on our lands."

"Much work has gone into what we have. We've put our hearts as well as our efforts into our homes," Quatie pointed out.

"And that is why I am working so hard to bring this unfairness to the attention of the federal government." John looked at G. W. "But, for now, we have no choice but to pack up the belongings we are allowed to take with us and move on. Some day, the Cherokee will receive the respect they deserve."

"Where will we go?" asked Silas nervously.

John Ross looked at his six-year-old son. "We'll go north, across the Tennessee line to Red Clay. Since the Cherokees are no longer allowed to have meetings in the state of Georgia, our capital at New Echota is practically useless. In Tennessee, the Cherokee Indians can hold meetings. There we can live peacefully in our homes like other American families."

"Doesn't the federal government care that you and 600 other Cherokees helped win the War of 1812?" Quatie asked.

John Ross shook his head. "President Andrew Jackson knows about it. But he seems to have a short memory."

October, 1835, Red Clay, Tennessee

John, Quatie, Silas, and G.W. Ross settled into the cabin at Red Clay, Tennessee. James and Allen were away attending school. John spent many hours recording the history and the constitution of the Cherokee Nation. He gathered the most thorough collection of written records of his people and their history. He became known as a leading authority on the Cherokee nation.

It was because of John's written records and knowledge of Cherokee history that John Payne wanted to meet John Ross. Payne was a journalist who had heard of the Indian removal problem while in Europe. He wanted to write stories about the plight of the Cherokee. Payne spent about three weeks at the Ross cabin copying records and legal documents and learning additional details about the Cherokee people from John Ross. Payne became enraged that the state of Georgia would not acknowledge the constitution of the Cherokee people nor grant them equal rights. He became more determined than ever to write newspaper stories about the situation.

Then one night, a shout sliced through the peaceful night. "Ross! Ross!"

John Ross locked eyes with his friend, the writer John Howard Payne. Who would be at the door at eleven o'clock at night? Both men glanced at little G. W. asleep on John Payne's lap. The noise had awakened Quatie, and she sat up in bed.

Before any of them could speak, another voice roared from the back door. Both doors burst open, and the one-room cabin was filled with armed men. Some were carrying rifles with bayonets, others had knives. Several had pistols drawn.

"Git over here against the wall with yore hands up!" one of the men bellowed.

"Make it quick!" another man snarled. "We don't have all night."

G. W. was wide awake now. He was trembling and clinging tightly to John Payne.

John Payne was the first to speak. "What are you doing? You have no right to barge into Chief Ross's home like this in the middle of the night. What do you want?"

"We've come to arrest Ross, but it jist might be that *you've* got what we want. Where's all those papers you been writin' for the newspapers? You been sayin' we're all a bunch of bandits takin' the Cherokee's Georgia land. You think that jist 'cause you're from the big city of New York that you know what we oughta be doin' in Georgia?" The man waved his pistol threateningly at Payne.

John Ross and John Payne moved back against the wall. Payne edged over toward the bed and handed G. W. to Quatie. Her frightened eyes glowed in the candlelight.

Several of the armed men began pawing through the papers stacked on the table. They frowned, picking up pages from one place and carelessly tossing them down in a different stack.

"Hey! You're getting my papers all out of order!" John Howard Payne ignored the man guarding him and started for the table. "I've spent weeks writing those!"

The guard slammed the barrel of his pistol across Payne's mouth. "Hold your cursed tongue! We'll decide what we want, and that's what we'll take!"

Blood spurted from Payne's lip, making splashes of brilliant red on his white shirt. Payne put his hand to his lip. In disbelief, he looked at the blood dripping between his fingers. His eyes scanned the half-circle of twenty-four men facing them. "Who are you people?"

The men laughed uproariously. "Why don't you ask your important friend there, Chief John Ross?" one asked.

Payne turned to Ross.

"You've heard me speak of the Georgia Guard? Well, here they are." Ross answered in a voice as cold as the Coosa River in January.

"What do you want with me?" Payne asked. "I'm not Cherokee."

"Might as well be," one of the men growled. "Sure on their side. That's why we're arresting you, too."

"Arresting me? What for?" Payne protested.

"For writin' all those fancy words about how the Cherokee are being treated unfairly." The man looked at Payne with a sneer. "Maybe we ought to make him move out west, too."

The men laughed as they prodded Ross and Payne with their bayonets out into the cold, rainy blackness of the night.

Little G. W. got down from the bed and went to the door. He opened it a crack and watched as the men on horseback took his father and Mr. Payne away. Turning to Quatie with tears in his eyes, G. W. said, "Ma, what did that man mean? Are we going to have to move again?"

Quatie frowned and walked over to G. W. She knelt down and put both her hands on his shoulders. "Some of the Cherokee have already moved out west. We may be forced to join them." Quatie's voice quivered as she spoke.

"Ma, what will happen to Pa?" G. W. asked.

"He is a brave and strong man, son, and I am not worried about him," said Quatie.

"Is Pa a good fighter, Ma?" G.W. asked.

"He fights brilliantly with words, son," Quatie said. "Why do you ask?"

"Because it took so many men with guns to arrest Pa and Mr. Payne," G. W. answered.

Two weeks later, a friend brought the Ross family a letter from John. It was dated October 25, 1835. "Please read it to us," Quatie said as she drew Silas and G.W. close to her.

He began to read slowly:

My dearest family, I pray that you are all well. John Payne and I were held at Spring Place in Georgia for nine long days. The Georgia Guard took us to the Joseph Vann house, another Cherokee home lost in the land lottery.

I was released today, but they refused to let John Payne come with me. I fear for my friend's health. He has never been subjected to such barbaric treatment. Their quarrel should not even be with him since he isn't a Cherokee.

I have tried to reassure him that it is only his writings about the Indian Removal situation that they are after. I believe that he will be released when they have examined and copied all his papers.

I will not rest until I know my friend John Payne is safe and free. This must be accomplished before I return home to you. I feel very sad to leave him still imprisoned. I fear the Georgia Guard will demand that he leave the state of Georgia and never return. For his own well-being, I hope he will do just that.

G.W., Mr. Payne wanted me to greet you especially. He said to tell you that when he had his paper and quills back, he would write to you. He said he will also continue to write articles exposing the injustices done to our people.

This cruel imprisonment has only strengthened my resolve. I will never stop trying to return the lands of the Cherokee to the hands of the rightful owners, our own people.

Thoughts of my family have been a source of strength to me. I will return home when my efforts here at Spring Place have resulted in John Payne's release.

Your loving father,

John Ross

THE TRAIL OF TEARS

John Howard Payne was released on October 29, 1835. After leaving Georgia, he spent time in Washington, D.C., writing articles for the Democratic Review. *In 1841, he began working for the War Department and continued writing about the Cherokees. Payne also wrote the lyrics for the ballad, "Home Sweet Home," which was the song most frequently sung by both the Union and Confederate soldiers around campfires during the Civil War.*

In 1838, John Ross finally admitted it was inevitable that the Cherokee would have to be removed to Indian Territory (in present-day Oklahoma). Ross was put in charge of the migration. Twelve detachments were set up, each group containing about a thousand people. Ross and his family traveled with the last detachment. There was great suffering and hardship on the long journey. Nearly a quarter of the tribe died on the way to the West during the winter of 1838–39. On the way, John Ross's wife, Quatie, gave her blanket to a sick child. The child recovered, but Quatie did not. She was buried on what has become known as the Trail of Tears. Many people consider these years to be the darkest in Georgia's history.

MAMMY KATE USES HER HEAD

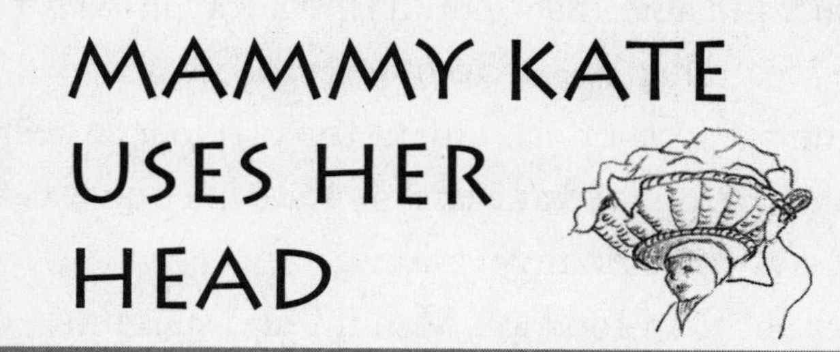

"Did you say she wants to starch my shirt?"

Stephen Heard stared at the guard, amazed. Ragged and filthy, Stephen had been held captive in the prison at Fort Cornwallis, Augusta, for days. He knew he would be hanged as soon as General Brown issued the order.

The guard nodded. "She's standing outside. Says the General gave her permission to see you."

The prisoner shrugged. Maybe there really was a washwoman waiting to see him.

As soon as she came down the stairs, Stephen recognized her. Even in the dim light of the prison, there was no mistake. This woman was a servant in his family's home. As tall as any man and stouter than most, the woman was wearing a white blouse that fairly gleamed against the rich brown of her skin. At the family home on Fishing Creek, Stephen and the other children had always called her Mammy Kate.

One look at Mammy Kate flooded the prisoner with memories. Scraped knees bathed by loving hands. Sweet ash cakes and warm kitchen fires. Clean linen starched into neat stacks. Mammy

Kate was strong, smart, and able. If she could find a way into Fort Cornwallis, Stephen Heard had reason to hope for a future.

Long years on the battlefront had taught the prisoner to keep his feelings off his face. He nodded at Mammy Kate like she was a stranger. "The guard says you'll do my washing."

"Yes, sir. I do washin'. Do a good job. Mendin' and starchin', too." She smiled down at the prisoner, showing a mouthful of white teeth. "You look like you could do with some mendin' right now!"

Stephen glanced at his ragged clothing. "Can you lend me a shirt until you clean up this one? I have a little money." He looked at Mammy Kate. Then he spoke the next words evenly. "I may as well spend my money now. I hear General Brown will order me hanged any day."

Mammy Kate handed a rough shirt to the prisoner. He slipped off his torn, soiled shirt and gave it to her. She dropped it into the large basket at her side.

"I'll be back tomorrow. Guess it won't do no good to put a clean shirt over that wound." She nodded at Stephen's shoulder. It was caked with blood and grime. "So I'll be bringin' a bucket to clean up that shoulder 'fore you put your shirt back on."

Stephen nodded again. He watched the guard show Mammy Kate up the stairs. Although his face betrayed no emotion, his heart pounded with joy. Mammy Kate would return tomorrow. If there was a way to escape from the British prison at Fort Cornwallis, he would live to tell about it.

Stephen Heard slept little that night. His shoulder pained him and his hunger woke him every hour or two.

When he dozed off, his sleep was full of horrible dreams—dreams of Jane, his young wife, forced out into the snow by British soldiers; visions of her bitter suffering, baby in her arms. In his dreams, Stephen kissed the baby's sweet and trusting face. He and Jane had adopted the baby, vowing to keep their child safe from harm. As he slept, Stephen lived through that terrible night with Jane. Through Jane's eyes, he watched their child freeze to death. Then he felt Jane's despair as she grew slowly colder. The child's lifeless body slipped out of her hands, and Jane sank down onto the snow. Mother and child were both dead, forced outside without blanket or shelter. Stephen relived his own pain, coming home from battle and finding them. How they must have called for him! And he had been far away, fighting for American freedom, too far away to save his own family.

For Stephen there was no comfort in sleeping. But tonight, for the first time, he was grateful for the pain. It kept him alert. Like a newly sharpened knife, his mind sliced through the problem: how could he escape?

Stephen Heard, age forty, was an officer in the Revolutionary Army. He had fought at the Battle of Kettle Creek. In the backcountry of Georgia, his name was linked with freedom fighters like Elijah Clarke, John Dooly, and John Twiggs.

After his capture, he had been put under heavy guard at Fort Cornwallis. General Brown was keeping him alive long enough to make a show of his hanging. His death would damage the spirit of the Whigs and serve as a warning to the rebellious farmers. Even the great General George Washington would grieve for Stephen Heard. They had fought together in the French and Indian Wars and held each other in high regard.

The British considered Heard a prize catch and they watched him carefully. How could he sneak out? The guards checked on him every hour. If he did manage to get out of the prison, he would still have to make his way out of the compound. That would be especially difficult since every British soldier in the fort knew his face.

Mammy Kate was the answer. In his heart, Stephen Heard knew she was his only chance. But how could she help him escape? She could report the location of the prison inside the fort. But what good would that do? How could a little band of patriots attack a heavily armed fort?

Perhaps Mammy Kate could smuggle a musket to Stephen? No, one armed man could never shoot his way out of this fort. Even with Mammy Kate reloading the musket at his side, it would be impossible. And Mammy Kate was not trained in fighting. She was large and strong, towering over Stephen. But even if she were a trained soldier, the two of them were no match for the whole British army.

Stephen was no closer to a solution when morning peeked through the cracks in his prison walls. His wound was growing worse for lack of treatment. The thin gruel he was fed twice a day barely softened his hunger. But he had trained his lean and wiry body to be commanded by his mind, and his mind was focused on one idea—escape.

Mammy Kate returned in the afternoon. The guard showed her down the stairs and remained by her side. Again, Stephen's face revealed no feelings. This time, Mammy Kate brought a bucket of water, some salve, and towels. As she cleaned his shoulder, she chatted about her success as a washwoman.

"Now I don't mind workin', that's for shore. And I see a whole lotta menfolk livin' at this here fort. They ain't got nobody to clean up their shirts. So I ask the guard at the gate do he want me to clean and starch his shirt. And I do a fine job for him.

"Pretty soon, I'm cleanin' and starchin' for all the guards at the gate. Then the officers start askin' me to do their shirts. And I'm glad to do that. But I tell them I charge a little bit more for them shirts with the ruffles.

"Then the Gen'ral himself asks me to do his shirt. And I'm real proud. But I tell him I'm gonna take extra time to press his shirt 'cause he's the most important British man in the fort. So I tell him I'll need a little bit more money.

"Well, that Gen'ral Brown, he laughs out real loud and says he wonders if I can wash as well as I can bargain. And I say the proof o' the puddin' is in the eatin'. When I bring him back his shirt, all white and pretty, he's real pleased. Yes, sir. Real pleased!"

Stephen listened as Mammy Kate bathed his wound. Gently, she picked out the stuck bits of fabric and dirt. Then she put a salve on the shoulder. As she worked, she talked and chuckled. It never occurred to the guard that the woman was giving an unusual amount of time to a stranger who was condemned to die.

At last, she put a bandage on the wound and handed Stephen

his clean and mended shirt. "Gen'ral Brown, he told me you won't be hangin' for a spell. So I guess I can make me some more money. I brung some old socks for you to wear. Now you give me that pair to wash. At least you'll be leaving this here place a clean man when your time comes!"

Mammy Kate emptied her bucket and placed it atop the soiled clothes in her basket. Then she nodded at the guard.

"You're doing a good business," the guard said. "That's the biggest basket I ever seen. And it's nearly full."

"Yes, sir!" said Mammy Kate, as she heaved the huge basket onto her head. "When most folks see the British army, they see a whole lotta muskets and uniforms. To me, it looks like a mighty good wash day!"

Stephen leaned against the wall and admired Mammy Kate's cunning. She had won the trust of these British soldiers. She'd found a way to get in and see him. She was making sure his wound would not prove another obstacle to his escape. But how could he escape? Mammy Kate would hear when General Brown planned to hang him. He had to have a plan ready.

He unrolled the rough socks Mammy Kate had lent him while she washed his own pair. There, in the middle of the roll was a square of ash cake! He popped it into his mouth, letting the sweet taste fill his mouth. Mammy Kate was a big woman with a big, stout heart!

Stephen sat down and tried to concentrate on a plan of escape. But his mind kept returning to the sight of Mammy Kate. Why, he'd wager the woman was stronger than two average men. That laundry basket was enormous. When it was full of clothes, it must have weighed as much as a young horse! And the woman plopped that load on her head like most folks would toss on a hat. Stephen smiled to himself. Ever since he was a boy, he had adored Mammy Kate. But now he had a new admiration for this brave and resourceful woman. If he ever got home, he vowed he'd give Mammy Kate her freedom.

The next afternoon dragged by. Stephen almost gave up hoping for another visit from Mammy Kate. But with the last light, she bustled in, basket by her side. Without a word, she handed him his socks in a roll. Stephen could feel a lump in the center. His mouth watered.

"I ain't got much time today. But I'd best see that shoulder."

Stephen slipped off his shirt and Mammy Kate dropped it into her basket. She unwrapped the bandage, bathed his wound, and rubbed it with salve. Then she put a clean bandage over it and handed him a clean shirt. The shoulder already looked much better.

Mammy Kate looked Stephen in the eyes. "Gen'ral Brown, he's ordered a hangin'. It'll be day after next." Stephen knew she was telling him to prepare to escape. "I've got me an old pair o' trousers, made outta sack. You put them on. I'm gonna wash up your pants and your shirt real good. This will be your last chance to get good and clean."

Stephen turned around. Quickly, he slipped off his trousers and put on the pair Mammy Kate had brought. She took his soiled clothes and laid them slowly in her huge basket. Then she looked at Stephen. With her eyes, she led him to look into the basket.

Stephen stared at Mammy Kate. There was no doubt about it. Her eyes were telling him about a plan of escape. She was planning to carry him out of the fort in her laundry basket!

He blinked. Surely, she was not thinking any such thought. Why, she could never carry a grown man inside that basket! She would stagger under the weight.

Stephen looked at Mammy Kate again. She was rearranging the clothes in the basket, showing him its depth. There was no doubt about it. The woman planned to carry Stephen Heard out of Fort Cornwallis on her head!

Mammy Kate bustled out of the prison. Stephen stood like a statue, weighing his alternatives. Either Mammy Kate would carry him out with the soiled laundry, or he would be hanged.

Stephen unwrapped the biscuit Mammy Kate had smuggled into his socks. She had even stuck a piece of salt pork in its center. Chewing slowly, he wondered how much he weighed. Always a small man, he was sure he had lost weight since his capture. He wondered how the weight of a man could be balanced on top of a head. He decided he would need to curl up in a ball. She might be able to do it if he could arrange his weight evenly in the bottom of the basket.

Stephen waited all of the next day for Mammy Kate to arrive. He paced up and down his cell. Had she been found out? He tried to see out the cracks in the wall. It was a clear afternoon and the air was turning crisp. The night would be chilly. Stephen pulled his uniform coat tight around the shirt Mammy Kate had lent him.

Would he ever see her again?

Suddenly, Stephen heard voices. Mammy Kate was coming down the stairs. The guard was talking to her. The man had a big smile on his face.

"I sure thank you. Haven't had a sweet as long as I can remember."

"I was glad to bring it. Just a little ash cake. Wish I had some more. One little cake don't hardly feed a passel o' soldiers." Mammy Kate grinned at the guard. "That ash cake shore tastes good warm from the oven."

The guard seemed eager to get back upstairs. Stephen guessed Mammy Kate had left the cake with the guards at the door.

As soon as they were alone, Mammy Kate put down her basket. From beneath a layer of clothes, she pulled out Stephen's shirt and pants. But they weren't starched and folded. His clothes were wrapped around a wad of stuffing. They were stuffed with other clothes into the shape of a person!

Quickly, Mammy Kate tugged at the sleeve of Stephen's coat. He slipped it off and helped her wrap it around the stuffed shirt. They laid the "body" on the floor of his cell. Then Mammy Kate pushed aside the linens in her basket, and Stephen climbed in. She covered him with clothes.

Stephen curled up on the bottom of the basket, trying to make his weight rest evenly against the sides. Suddenly, he felt himself lifted into the air. For a second, the basket teetered. He shifted a bit, and the bundle settled on Mammy Kate's head. Stephen lay quietly as Mammy Kate climbed the stairs. With every step, he felt the basket heave. But the woman did not grunt or strain.

"Done already?" asked the guard.

"Reckon I've done as much as I can for him," said Mammy Kate. "Guess he's as ready for his long journey as the likes of me can make him."

"This cake is quite good," said one of the soldiers. "I thank you for bringing it."

"You come back tomorrow," said another of the guards. "I'll have more washing to give you."

Mammy Kate walked slowly through the fort. Many of the British soldiers called out to her. She had a pleasant, unhurried word for every man in the fort. Stephen held his breath every time Mammy Kate stopped to visit. But he knew she had to appear calm or the soldiers might suspect something. He wondered how long it would be before before his guard brought supper to the prisoner. If Mammy Kate and her laundry basket hadn't reached the walls of the fort before Stephen was found missing, all was lost.

"Washwoman, halt!" thundered a voice. Mammy Kate turned slowly. Stephen held a rag in front of his mouth to muffle his breathing.

A man came running. He was breathing hard. "The General wants you to come get some shirts."

Mammy Kate spoke slowly. "These British men have given me as much as I can carry. You tell Gen'ral Brown I'll come back. Shore 'nuff I'll be back—as shore as the British army is the finest in this land!"

Mammy Kate smiled a large, wise smile at the soldier. "One thing don't need no hurryin' is the wash. Dirty clothes ain't gonna run away from your Fort Cornwallis!"

The soldier laughed. "I suppose you're right." He winked at Mammy Kate. "I'll tell the General you left the fort before I could catch you."

The soldier walked away, chuckling. He called back to Mammy Kate. "I'll tell General Brown not to worry. His shirts will still be dirty tomorrow'"

It was dusk when Mammy Kate reached the walls of the fort. One of the soldiers at the gate tipped his hat to her. "That basket looks heavier than usual today. Need a hand carrying it?"

'No sir," laughed Mammy Kate. "Got me this head. Don't need no soldier's hands!"

"I think you'll be busy tonight. That's a lot of laundry," said the soldier.

"You know what

they say," said Mammy Kate. "Idle hands do the devil's work. So I shore am thankful these hands are full of laundry. That keeps them outta trouble."

Mammy Kate hummed to herself as she walked through the gates of Fort Cornwallis. Keeping her slow pace, she walked down the path through the trees. At last, the fort could not be seen through the foliage. She heaved the great basket onto the ground. She pushed aside the laundry, and Stephen jumped out. Mammy Kate concealed the basket in the undergrowth. Then she led Stephen along a narrow deer trail to a clearing where two horses stood waiting.

Without a word, they untied the horses, mounted them, and rode away through the forest. They traveled hard for two hours. When they came in sight of some barns owned by one of the freedom fighters, they knew they were safe.

Mammy Kate turned to Stephen, looking at him closely. "Master Stephen, I declare you are thinner than you was when you was a youngun. Mammy Kate's gonna have plenty of cookin' to do when we get back to Fishin' Creek."

Stephen grinned. "I'm looking forward to it." Then he became serious. "Mammy Kate, you freed me from the British. As soon as this backcountry is safe for travel, I plan to set you free."

"Master Stephen, you can make Mammy Kate free o' you if you want." She gave a great, warm laugh. "But in his heart, Master Stephen ain't never gonna get free o' his Mammy Kate!"

STEPHEN AND MAMMY KATE AFTER THE WAR

The story of Stephen Heard's escape from Fort Cornwallis in Mammy Kate's laundry basket was handed down from generation to generation in the Heard family. Heard lived about forty-five miles from Augusta, fought at the battle of Kettle Creek, and lost his first wife and adopted child to the cruelty of the British army. In September of 1780, he was imprisoned in the British prison at Fort Cornwallis.

Heard was a respected patriot who served briefly as acting governor of Georgia. For many years, he was a county representative to the Georgia Assembly. He did remarry and had nine children with his second wife. He built a grand estate named Heardmont, which was once considered the finest house north of Augusta. He died in 1815 at the age of seventy-five. When Heard County was created in 1830, it was named in honor of this Revolutionary War hero and prominent citizen.

Although Heard's house at Heardmont is no longer standing, the family cemetery can still be seen. The graves of Stephen Heard and several members of his family are clearly marked inside the walled family plot. Nearby is the grave of Mammy Kate.

WAR WOMAN

First, there came a fierce pounding. Then a hoarse voice demanded, "Open this door or we'll bust it in!"

Sukey stood in the shadows, watching. It was the nightmare she'd had over and over during months of fighting in the north Georgia backcountry. The nightmare came more often as death came closer to their cabin door. Only a few weeks had passed since their neighbor, brave John Dooly, had heard the pounding. His wife had opened their cabin door that black night, and the Tories had murdered John Dooly before he could push aside his bedcovers. They shot him in front of his wife and his children.

Now the Tories were standing outside the Hart cabin. Sukey's mother straightened her back and threw open the door.

"This be the Hart cabin?" the voice shot through the door.

"It be," replied Nancy Hart. "And you'll not find a welcome for Tories here."

Sukey swallowed her breath. Her mother stood six feet tall. Every inch of her was tough as leather and hard as nails. The child braced herself for the sound of the musket that would silence her mother's voice.

Instead, she heard a man ask, "Be you the wife of Ben Hart? The woman the rebels call Aunt Nancy?"

Again Sukey held her breath. If only her mother would lie. She could say she was a neighbor-woman or a visitor. What would the Tories do to the wife of an officer in the Revolutionary Army? To the healer they called Aunt Nancy? Surely they would kill her.

Without so much as a blink of her piercing blue eyes, Sukey's mother spoke. "I am Nancy Hart. Ben Hart is my husband." The tall woman's hair blazed red in the afternoon light.

"There's a matter we have to discuss with your husband. A man escaped from our soldiers by this cabin door. There are serious consequences for those who give aid to the enemies of the King."

"You'll not be needing to see my Ben," announced Nancy. "I can tell the tale. A man came riding out of yonder trees day before yesterday. He was chased by a bloodthirsty pack of men who obey a cruel tyrant. I know this man that your soldiers chased. He's a good man who loves the name of liberty. If he was your fox, then the men who chased him were foolish hounds. What a pretty tale I have to tell of his escape from foolish soldiers easily turned from the chase!" She gave a great laugh, but there was nothing merry in her voice.

Sukey strained to hear the sound of riders. If only her father and his band of patriots would return while Nancy was speaking to the Tory soldiers! Sukey craned her neck to count the soldiers. She counted five of them—not too many for Ben and his men to capture.

Nancy continued the story: "The man ran up to this yard and

called out to me. I took down a rail from the fence and bid him ride up to this door. Then I urged his horse through the door, and he rode right through this cabin and out the back door."

Sukey glanced at the back door. Their cabin was one big room. When both of the doors were open, a man could go in the front and out the back in seven strides. Sukey longed to sneak out the back door and get help. But she knew the Tories would see her. She would be caught, maybe shot, before she reached the swamp.

Nancy gestured at the doors. "There's been a rain since the man ran through this door, and the swamp goes back a piece. But I can't stop you if you've a notion to try and find the man's trail." Nancy planted her muscular arms upon her hips and sneered at the men. "Of course, it would have been easier to follow his trail the day before yesterday. If Your Majesty's men hadn't been so peacock-proud, you'd have the man's hide stretched and tanned by now."

Nancy threw back her head and crowed proudly, "You would'a thought the fools might'a read the tracks in the muck outside the door! Or had a look at the muddy tracks right across this floor. But no, the peacocks come a'knocking at this door, all puffed up with their importance. And here I was all flushed from heaving the rail back in place and rushing to bolt the cabin doors. I covered up my head, so." Nancy threw her scarf over her head to demonstrate. "Then I stooped over and hobbled to unbolt the door. And I said, 'I'm just a sick, lone woman. Why are you disturbing me?' And the peacocks asked me had I seen a man on horseback. So I said he went down the road yonder. And then the whole kit and kaboodle went galloping off without checking for a single hoofprint on the road.

"So there's your tale. But I've no more time to tell stories today. You Tories have stripped the very weeds from our fields. We country folk can scarce find a scrap for our table." With that, Nancy turned to shut the cabin door.

A Tory who stood in the rear of the group hollered, "Can you cook as well as you brag, rebel woman?"

Sukey was only eleven, but she could guess what these men had in mind. They had tried to scare her mother into lying or pleading for her life. But instead, Nancy had shamed them by bragging about how she'd helped a rebel escape. How foolish she made the soldiers look! How could five men gun down an unarmed, unafraid woman?

Now the Tories were demanding to be fed. Everyone in these parts knew how Nancy Hart felt about Tories. She was a proud patriot, and she despised the men who bowed to the King of England. She would die before she'd agree to cook for them! Sukey was terrified. She was sure the soldiers were looking for an excuse to kill her mother. If Nancy Hart refused an order to feed them, they would have their excuse. They'd hang her mother as a rebel.

Sukey had to do something. She rushed from the shadows and blurted out, "My mother is the best cook in Georgia. She can cook a pumpkin as many ways as there are days in the week."

Nancy scowled at her daughter. "Child, a body can't cook what isn't there. These Tories have stolen every living thing from forest and field."

At this, the Tory in the rear cupped his hands and yelled, "I see a bird over there. You can cook him for our dinner, Aunt Nancy."

Before Nancy could speak, the man raised his musket and shot the Hart's old tom turkey. He was the last of their toms, and there would be no more young turkeys for their table, thought Sukey.

The soldier ran over to the dead fowl and grabbed its legs. He heaved it at Nancy's feet. All five of the men pushed their way into the cabin. They flopped down on the rough benches and stools like they owned the place.

Sukey watched her mother's face. When Nancy Hart scowled, her eyes narrowed and her gaze grew intense. She looked like a hawk that had just caught sight of a mouse.

Then Nancy gave Sukey a meaningful look. "Child, go fetch me a bucket of water from the spring. And make haste. Take the path by the hollow stump. I look for you to be back in two blows of a horn. I've got me a bird to pluck, some smoked venison I mean to stew, and hoecakes with honey to set out. If I'm going to feed the King's men, I'm going to see to it they'll never get a better meal." And with that, she handed Sukey the small bucket and pushed her out the door.

Sukey headed for the spring. What did her mother mean for her to do? Surely Nancy Hart did not intend to make a feast for the Tories? And why did she say to take the path by the hollow stump? That way took much longer. Maybe her mother was so nervous she forgot which way was shorter?

No, that didn't make a bit of sense, Sukey thought as she hurried along the path. Nancy Hart was the bravest woman in Georgia.

The Indians even had a nickname for her—War Woman. Hadn't Nancy dressed as a man and wandered alone through the enemy camp, pretending to be crazy? She had kept her wits about her and brought back reports about the number of enemy troops, amounts of ammunition, and attack plans. Her mother had once fashioned a raft of logs held together with grapevines to cross a swollen river and spy on Loyalists. When the patriots pushed back the Tories at the famous Battle of Kettle Creek, Nancy Hart was there, fighting right beside her husband and oldest son. Why, General Clarke himself said that Aunt Nancy was the best secret weapon the patriots had in the backcountry!

Sukey took the long way by the hollow stump. She walked quickly because her mother had bid her to make haste. As she came near the stump, she remembered her mother's words. Nancy had told Sukey to be back in two blows of a horn. That was it!

Sukey reached inside the stump and pulled out the conch shell the Harts kept inside the hollow wood. Two blows on the shell was the signal they used to call the militia. Two blows meant get your arms and ride close. Sukey put the shell to her lips and sounded it twice.

But why shouldn't she blow the conch a third time? Three blows meant to begin attack. Sukey raised the conch to give the third blow. But she hesitated. Her mother had said, "Be back in *two* blows." Her mother must have a plan.

Quickly, Sukey replaced the conch. She ran down to the spring and filled the small bucket. Then she took the shortcut back to the cabin. Her mother had a plan! And she needed Sukey's help!

Sukey's eyes grew wide as she opened the cabin door. There was her mother sweating as she hastily stuffed the fowl. She had already stoked up the fire. The room was warm, and the smell of cooking venison filled the air. The Tories had their feet up on stools, smoking. One of the men was taking a swig from a jug. Amazed, Sukey watched the Tory stand up and hand the jug to Nancy. Sukey had seen her mother drink whiskey like a man. But here was Aunt Nancy the patriot sharing a jug with a band of Tories!

"Don't be standing there, child," Nancy said to Sukey. "Bring the water and mix up the batter for hoecakes."

Sukey set to work. She was full of questions that she dared not ask. As she bustled around the table, she listened to all the conversations. She noticed that the men had piled their muskets in the corner, like company come to dinner.

"Well, he was plenty angry when we come back from them canebrakes empty-handed!" one of the Tories was saying. "At first, he thought we was lying. He made us stand stiff at attention to see if our bellies looked stuffed. Now does that make sense? How could a handful of men eat up all that stock? But it sure looked bad for awhile. It's a court-martial for stealing provisions from the army."

Sukey watched her mother's face. Had she heard the man talking? Why, it was Nancy Hart who had found the stolen animals grazing on the river's islands. Nancy was a skilled hunter, and she supplied most of the meat for the Harts' table. She was out hunting when she spotted the missing livestock grazing in the canebrakes. She told Colonel Dooly, and the militia took a raft out to the islands to get the stock. After all, the animals belonged to the farmers in these parts. The farmers hadn't fattened up their stock to feed a tyrant's army!

The patriots said that John Dooly was murdered because of the raid on the livestock. The Tories were planning to send the stock to their army in Augusta, badly in need of food. But John Dooly didn't deserve to be shot for taking those animals. The Tories were the ones who stole them in the first place.

"Sukey, look lively," Nancy said. "Stir the stew so's it doesn't burn."

Three of the Tories were taking turns at arm wrestling at the Harts' rough table. Nancy covered up the roasting fowl. Then she sat down on a stool by the arm wrestlers. She propped her elbow across from one of the men and nodded. The man laughed at the offer, but he grabbed Nancy's arm and tried to force it down with one mighty push. Her arm did not budge.

"Ho, Aaron's no match for an auntie!" whooped the man beside him. The other Tories turned to look.

Nancy scowled at her opponent. He tried to stare her down, but he couldn't hold his gaze. His arm was starting to tremble. He grunted and swore. Then he watched his arm slam against the rough boards. "Corn whiskey must'a put the devil into you, rebel woman," the man said. "I ain't never seen a woman can outwrestle a man!"

"Maybe corn whiskey took the devil outta you, Aaron," laughed another of the Tories. This man brushed Aaron off the stool and sat down. He was the heaviest man in the group. Sukey thought he was the leader by the way he talked.

The leader was a better match for Nancy. The veins bulged on the man's arm as he pushed against Nancy's arm. Finally, slowly, he pinned her arm. The man let his arm drop to his lap and rubbed it vigorously.

Nancy kept her elbow on the table and the scowl on her face. "Two outta three," she said.

The leader cursed, but he replaced his elbow on the table. This time, it was no contest. The man's forehead was drenched in sweat. His arm trembled violently. Nancy flattened his hand against the table. The man shook his head and let his arm drop by his side. But Nancy kept her arm on the table. So the man propped up his arm a third time. Nancy brought it down with a thud.

The man mopped his forehead with his sleeve. "Whew! I sure hope you can cook like you can wrestle, woman. I ain't never knowed a man who could pin my arm."

Nancy whooped. "You're strong enough, I guess. Only one man's ever pinned down my arm every time. And that was my daddy!"

"Your husband, can he beat you?" asked the Tory named Aaron.

"Yep. Ben's a poor ol' stick. But he can always best me on the first try. 'Course I can pin him two outta every three. I once knew another man could best my arm on the first try. And he was the bravest man I ever met in these parts."

Sukey looked at her mother's face. For a moment, it looked as if Nancy would cry. That man who could match her at arm-wrestling was John Dooly. He had been a good neighbor and a devoted patriot. His death was a blow to the backcountry freedom fighters.

Nancy pushed her stool under the table. She picked up the basket of turkey feathers and handed them to Sukey. "Put these feathers in the sack out back, child."

"But, mother..." Sukey started to protest. They kept the sack of feathers tied below the rafters. What could her mother mean?

Nancy gripped her daughter's shoulders and looked her straight in the eyes. "Out back, Sukey. By the pecan tree," she said flatly.

Sukey took the basket out the back door of the cabin. She looked for a sack by the pecan tree. She turned around and around, searching. Then she saw the musket! The muzzle of one of the Tory muskets was poking out of the chink between the logs of the cabin wall. That's why her mother had told Sukey to go out back! Quickly, Sukey grasped the musket and pulled it through the crack. It was followed by a second musket. She laid them down and covered them with an old horse blanket. Then she emptied the feathers into a crate and scrambled back inside the cabin.

Nancy had her apron full of apples, and she was placing the fruit on the table. So that's how her mother had managed to push the guns out the chink in the wall! Nancy must have sweet-talked the soldiers into piling their muskets in that corner while Sukey was fetching the water. Her mother knew there were gaping cracks between the logs in that wall. Ben would patch the cracks with river clay when the cold weather set in.

As soon as Sukey took the turkey feathers outside, Nancy had gone to that corner and stooped down to gather apples from the basket kept there. With her back to the Tories, Nancy had smuggled out two of the muskets to Sukey's waiting hands.

So that was Nancy Hart's plan! She had tricked the soldiers. She had lulled their fears with the smells of good food. She had welcomed their liquor into her cabin. And they had set aside their weapons. Aunt Nancy, the rebel, was going to deliver them, drunk and unarmed, to Ben's troop.

Sukey was setting the table when the Tories mentioned John Dooly. The stout Tory with the mustache, flushed with the heat of the cabin and the whiskey, boasted, "That rebel, he looked me straight in the eye, he did. And he made to speak. I shot before he could say a word."

"You weren't supposed to shoot him, Zeb," said the smallest man in the band. "Leastways not 'til he admitted he'd done the raid on the stock. We was sent to question the man."

Zeb shrugged, brushing aside the criticism. "And when he said he stole the stock, we was gonna hang him. Hang him or shoot him, what's it matter? We was told to make John Dooly an example for any other thievin' rebel."

"Seems to me the man should'a been questioned first," persisted the small man. "And we shouldn't have shot John Dooly in his bed."

Another Tory snorted. "Well, at least he died comfortable! That's more than a rebel deserves."

The leader spoke up. "Henry's right, Zeb. Dooly should'a been given a chance to say his prayers 'fore we killed him. And a chance to say the names of the other rebels who needed hanging on the same rope!"

Sukey lowered her eyes and stole a glance at her mother. Everyone said Aunt Nancy's face was easier to read than the pages of a book. But Sukey couldn't read her mother's thoughts today. Had she heard the Tories laughing about the murder of brave John Dooly?

Nancy handed Sukey the bucket. Smiling, she said, "Go fetch some more water for our guests to drink. We're ready to serve His Majesty's men the best meal they'll ever get. Make haste, child. I look for you in three blows of a horn."

Sukey nodded at her mother. Now she understood exactly what her mother was telling her. She was to blow three times on the conch to call Ben Hart and his men to come and capture the Tories.

Sukey fairly flew to the hollow stump. No wonder her mother had given her the small bucket to fill on her first trip. Nancy knew she would have to send Sukey back to the stump, back to blow the conch shell. Sukey gave three great blows on the conch, praying her father was nearby and would hear the signal. Then Sukey gasped. What if the Tories heard the sound? Would they realize they had been tricked? Sukey filled the bucket with water and raced back to the cabin.

As she came running up the path, she shouted, "Here I come, Mother. As quick as three blows of a horn!"

Nancy threw open the cabin door and took the bucket. "Sukey, bring another log for the fire." She pointed to the spot where she had passed the muskets through the chink between the logs.

Sukey stood ready to catch the guns, her heart pounding with the danger. How long would it take her father to reach the cabin?

Then she heard a commotion inside, and her heart froze.

"What are you doing with that musket, rebel woman?" shouted one of the Tories.

They had caught her mother passing the gun out to Sukey!

"Stand where you are," thundered Nancy Hart. "I'll blow out the brains of the first man who moves."

Sukey heard a scuffle. Then the terrible blast of a musket split the air. There was a loud thud and confused voices.

Quicker than lightning, Sukey scooped up one of the muskets at her feet. She scrambled into the cabin and passed it to Nancy. At her mother's feet, the Tory named Zeb lay in a heap.

"Another man moves, another Tory dies," Nancy said. "Have you signalled to the militia, child?"

"Yes, mother. Papa and them will be here soon."

The Tories looked at each other. Fear was written across their faces. If they rushed Nancy, they had a chance. But she was a fine marksman. The Tory named Zeb had just forfeited his life to prove her skill. And the way she scowled at all of them! It was impossible to tell which man she was aiming at.

The leader took a cautious step forward. Nancy shot him in the leg. He collapsed, groaning. Sukey picked up a fresh musket from the guns stacked against the wall and handed it to her mother. The other three Tories eyed each other and Nancy. They dared not move.

The heat in the cabin seemed to press upon Sukey. The Tories stood stiff as statues. Only their eyes seemed alive. Each man watched Nancy, looking for a chance to spring. But her hawk's glare was impossible to read. Each man thought she was aiming the musket at him.

Finally, Sukey heard the sound of the riders. Sukey wanted to run out to her father. But she knew better than to move from Nancy's side. If a Tory made a dash for the door, her mother would fire the musket. Sukey would have to hand Nancy a loaded gun before another Tory could move.

Ben Hart burst into the cabin, surrounded by his band of patriots. "Well, this is a pretty sight! Nancy's cooking dinner. And we've been called to feast on some Tories!"

"What should we do with 'em, Ben?" asked one of the patriots. "I say we march 'em outside and shoot 'em."

"Shooting's too good for the bunch that murdered John Dooly," declared Nancy. "I say take 'em out back and hang 'em."

So the patriots marched the four Tories out of the cabin. One of Ben's men picked up the dead Tory and slung him across his shoulders. Nancy Hart led the way to the big oak tree, a musket in her arms. As she walked, she whistled the tune "Yankee Doodle."

MORE ABOUT THE WILD WAR WOMAN

Nancy Hart lived in the part of Georgia that is now Elbert County for about twenty years. She was the wife of Benjamin Hart and mother of six sons and two daughters. The events in this story took place during the Revolutionary War, during the summer of 1780 when savage fighting was going on in the Georgia and Carolina backcountry.

When Hart County was created in 1853, it was named for this Revolutionary War heroine. She is the only woman to have a Georgia county named in her honor. There is also a Hart State Park and Nancy Hart Highway. A replica of her log cabin can be found near the Broad River at what is believed to be the site of the Hart homestead.

The "patriots" in this story refer to those colonists who fought for or supported independence from England. The colonists who supported the King of England's right to govern the American colonies were called "Tories" or "Loyalists." The colonists often called the British soldiers "redcoats" because of their bright scarlet uniforms.

ESCAPE FROM BLACKBEARD ISLAND

At the touch of metal against his skin, Andrew Henson's eyes shot open. In the dim light of morning, the boy focused on a large and oily nose. The stink of the man's breath was so terrible that Andrew nearly got sick. Then pain shocked him fully awake. A knife. The man had poked Andrew with the blade of a knife! Andrew jumped up, slamming into another man.

Now a large, hairy arm locked around Andrew's neck. The boy tried to twist away. The arm held him fast. Andrew thought the arm would stop his breathing. He strained and struggled.

Suddenly, the man with the knife gestured. The man with the hairy arm let go of Andrew. Then the two men looked the boy up and down.

"An English boy, ain't ye?"

"Yes, sir," Andrew said.

"Live in the colonies?" asked the man with the knife.

"Yes, sir. On the mainland. The colony of Georgia."

"Why are ye sleeping alone out here?"

Andrew was too scared to lie. "I ran away, sir." He was sorry as soon as he said the words. "My stepfather is a hard man." Andrew held his breath.

The men looked at each other. "How'd ye come here from the mainland?"

"On a boat. With some of the fellows who work for my stepfather. We needed to brand the calves. You see, my stepfather keeps cattle on Sapelo. He has grazing rights on the island." Andrew's face showed his disgust. He hated the cattle. For that matter, he hated everything about farming—it was pure drudgery, in Andrew's opinion. His own father had been a seaman. And that was the life Andrew was sure he was meant for.

The man with the knife leered at the boy. "So a farmer's life don't suit ye, eh?"

"That's right, sir. I'm looking for the beach where the pirate ships come ashore. I aim to join a pirate ship."

Andrew had no sooner uttered these words than the men roared with laughter.

Andrew studied the men. They were dressed in stained pants and leather shoes. Their baggy shirts hung open at the neck. He could see their muscles bulging under their clothes. Andrew noticed that their faces were tanned and leathery. Both of them were unshaven, and their greasy hair hung down past their shoulders. The man with the knife had a scar on his neck. The man with the hairy arm wore a strip of bright cloth tied around his forehead.

These men work hard, Andrew thought. They work outdoors in the sun and wind. Why, these men look exactly like pirates!

Andrew blurted out, "Are you pirates?"

The men stared at him.

"Please," he stammered. "If you are, might I join your crew?"

The men burst into laughter again. Then Hairy Arm grabbed the back of Andrew's collar. Half dragging, he led Andrew into the trees.

"Won't ol' Teach have a time when we tell him this tale!" said the man with the hairy arm.

Both men laughed again. Then they eyed each other. The man with the knife spoke. "Could be ol' Teach ain't in a merry way this mornin'. Cap'n was in his cups till last watch."

"You don't think the Captain will allow me on board?" asked Andrew.

Hairy Arm said, "The Cap'n, he has his own ideas. He don't take to strangers."

The man with the knife sneered. "Mebbe ol' Teach would take more kindly to a boy that knew a sailing ship."

The remark stung Andrew. He knew nothing of ships, but his father had been a seaman all his life. Andrew believed he would take to a seagoing life as a seagull takes to flying. "I don't mind," Andrew said politely. "If your captain won't take me, I'll wait for another ship. It's only November. I can take care of myself until another ship comes by."

The men eyed each other. Then Hairy Arm spoke: "I suppose ye'd tell the next ship where we found ye."

Andrew nodded agreeably.

The man with the knife scowled. "Ol' Teach says dead men don't tell tales."

Hairy Arm rubbed his chin thoughtfully. Then he spit out a

stream of brown liquid. "I say we give the lad a chance. Ship needs a boy. This one's got some spirit. And he's willin'. We had to blindfold and drag the last one."

The man with the knife nodded. Then he dug a coin out of his pocket. "We'll toss for the man who carries the tale to Cap'n," he said. "Heads and the chore is yours. Tails—I tell the tale."

Hairy Arm grinned in reply. The man with the knife tossed the coin in the air. Then he opened his hand. The coin showed a head.

Hairy Arm swore. "Telling this tale may cost me an ear. Or worse," he growled.

"Let the boy wait in the trees by the beach," said the man with the knife. "If the Cap'n's head is clear, show him the lad. If he's full of rum, mind your counsel. Ye can show him the lad after we set sail."

The men strode off in silence, dragging Andrew along. Hairy Arm held the boy's collar firmly. Andrew knew something had gone wrong. He had offered to join the pirates, but now he was a captive, not a volunteer.

They made their way into a dense forest. Walking was difficult through the sharp palmetto leaves and the tangled vines. Gnarled trees, covered with shaggy coats of lichen and dripping with Spanish moss, loomed all around them. The pirates pulled Andrew along between them, ignoring the roots that seemed to grab at the boy's feet.

Andrew wondered where they were. He knew he had traveled east last night. He had walked for miles through the pastures and forests on Sapelo Island. At dusk he had come to a marsh. He had waded through the muck and splashed across a salty creek. Then he had trudged through another mile of marsh. When at last his feet had struck firm ground, the blackness was so complete that he could not see his hand before his face. He wondered if he was still on Sapelo. Perhaps he had blundered onto another island.

Without knowing why, Andrew brought his voice down to a whisper. "What is the name of this island?"

Hairy Arm shrugged. "They call it Blackbeard Island."

Andrew shivered as if a cold wind had blown across his parched skin. His mind began to race. He had heard of a pirate called Blackbeard. Why, Blackbeard's crimes were famous down the whole length of the Atlantic colonies! It was said he once held the city of Charleston at ransom. Blackbeard sometimes showed kindness to the people he captured, and sometimes he cut them down like sheaves of wheat. At the sound of his name, sea captains gave up their ships without a fight. Merchants opened their warehouses and let Blackbeard's crew grab whatever they wished.

Andrew stopped. "You called this Blackbeard Island?"

Hairy Arm nodded.

"Is it Blackbeard's ship you sail on? Is that who your Captain Teach is?"

"Aye. He's the famous Blackbeard, all right." Hairy Arm spoke in a dead voice. Andrew wondered why the man did not roar with laughter at the fame of his captain.

Again the trio walked in silence. Andrew thought they were following a path of sorts. Perhaps the brush had been worn down by the deer that roamed the islands. Andrew wished the men would boast or laugh. Or just speak. Why was he getting so nervous? This was what he came to find, wasn't it? He was going to join a pirate ship and become a seaman like his father.

As the sun rose, the air became hot and close in the forest. Andrew was sweating so heavily that his shirt grew limp. His pant legs, as stiff as sandpaper from the dried salt water, scratched his legs as he walked. Swarms of insects stung Andrew and buzzed around his face. Andrew had not eaten or had a drink since sundown, and he was starting to feel light-headed.

But of all his discomforts, the smell was the worst. A rancid odor that reminded Andrew of vinegar and rotting garbage grew stronger as the sun grew hotter. The skin of the men oozed with the smell. The smell attracted clouds of gnats that swirled around the pirates' heads. They swatted at the tiny black specks, swearing horrible oaths. Andrew had never heard such foul curses.

The boy tried to think. Could these men be trusted or would they turn violent? Perhaps he should try to trick them and slip away? His thoughts kept straying. He could not decide what to do. Instead, he found himself dwelling on the wretched smell, the foul sounds, the itching, the hunger.

At last, the forest began to thin out, and Andrew could hear the roar of the surf. Hairy Arm gripped the boy's shirt collar tightly. Andrew did not make a sound. He knew they were coming near to the pirate ship.

The men stopped at the edge of the forest. Before them stretched a narrow beach and then the open ocean. A large wooden ship was lying on its side at the edge of the water. It rolled and bobbed in the breaking waves. Men swarmed over it, slipping off and climbing back onto its rounded hull. Some of the men were naked. Others wore clothes, but they were soaking wet. The men were scraping the ship's boards that usually rode under the water. Andrew had heard of this. It was called "careening." The crew was scraping off barnacles. They were working quickly so they could flip the heavy ship to an upright position with the help of the incoming tide.

Hairy Arm pulled Andrew over to a tree with low, spreading branches. He hoisted the boy onto a limb, seating him as if he were astride a horse. The men took out their knives and freed two long vines. They tied one vine firmly around Andrew's ankles. Then they held the boy's arms behind his back and tied together his wrists.

Next, Hairy Arm fished a coin out of his pants. He showed it to Andrew. The golden coin was not quite round. It had a picture on it that Andrew had not seen on any English coin. Hairy Arm held the coin in front of Andrew's face. When he was sure he had the boy's attention, he put the coin between his own teeth and bit down. Then he put the coin between Andrew's teeth and nodded. Andrew also bit down. Hairy Arm held the coin before Andrew's eyes to show him the dents their teeth had made. Both men grinned, then Hairy Arm put the coin between Andrew's lips, ruffled the boy's hair, and waved goodbye.

Andrew watched the men amble down the beach, waving to their mates. He could holler if he spit out the coin, but he didn't want to lose it in the dense plant growth. Andrew knew the coin was very valuable. It must be pure gold because it was easily dented by teeth. The pirates had given him this coin to keep him quiet.

Andrew saw the men join the others at the edge of the ocean. He did not trust them. Why had they tied him up and bought his silence with a gold coin? Perhaps the life of a boy on a pirate ship was not as exciting as he had imagined. Andrew remembered what Hairy Arm had said about the last ship's boy: he had to be blindfolded and dragged aboard. Andrew tried to reassure himself. He was, after all, a boy with spirit. He was not weak and timid like some boys. Andrew was sure his bravery would impress the pirates. Before long, he thought, he'd be in command of his own ship. And be rich, to boot! Why, these pirates probably had chests full of gold coins like the one Andrew was holding in his lips.

Hairy Arm and the man with the knife kicked off their boots as they reached the edge of the water. They waded and swam up to the ship and began to scrape at its boards. As Andrew watched, he wiggled his hands and feet. The vine slipped up and down. The pirates had not stripped off the bark. Andrew found he could loosen the vine by making it rub against itself, removing the bark. Finally, Andrew was able to pull out one hand. He unwrapped his other hand and his feet. He took the coin from his mouth, kissed it for good luck, and tied it carefully in the hem of his shirt.

The tide was coming in fast. Andrew could no longer hear the men's voices over the crash of waves. The great ship was heaving with each wave, straining to stand upright. At last, Andrew saw the pirates jump into the water. They swam out from the vast hull, riding waves to the beach. The crew lined up on the shore, water streaming off them. They took places along three thick ropes that led down the beach, disappearing under the foam. Then the lines of men walked, straining and tugging at the ropes, toward Andrew. Andrew crouched behind the tree, watching. The men pulled hard, their feet digging into the soft sand. At last, the great ship swung up from the seas with a smacking sound. The men's roar momentarily drowned out the roar of the surf. Then they ran down the beach. In an instant, the beach was a riot of motion—men loading crates, coiling ropes, bustling back and forth.

All of Andrew's doubts were forgotten as he watched the proud ship being readied for sailing. He waited for the best moment to march out of the shade and announce himself to the captain. But which of the men was Blackbeard? Andrew squinted. He could not pick out any man who seemed to be in command. Perhaps a pirate crew was a collection of equals, Andrew thought. Perhaps every man did his work without being bossed by a captain. Perhaps this Captain Blackbeard was an easygoing chap when he wasn't drinking rum!

Suddenly, all activity on the beach stopped. The men stood still, the seawater swirling around their feet. It was as if a painting had replaced the living scene. All of the pirates were looking at a spot to Andrew's right. But the sand dunes prevented Andrew from following the men's gaze.

Quickly, Andrew swung himself back up onto the branch and managed to find a steady perch. Now he could follow the men's eyes. There, walking along the edge of the surf was a tall man with smoke curling out of his thick black beard. The man looked like a human volcano!

Andrew watched the man approach the pirates. He stood at least a head taller than the others. He was dressed like the other pirates, except his shirt was unbuttoned all the way to his waist. Dotted here and there through his black beard were little bits of red fabric. Smoke swirled around the man's face and formed small clouds on his beard.

Surely, the tall man was on fire! Why didn't he leap into the sea to put out the blaze? Why didn't the others run to his aid with buckets of water? Andrew could not stop staring. The human volcano began waving his arms around. Horrified, Andrew saw that he was holding a pistol in each hand. Was this a bandit, come to rob the pirates of their gold?

Then the man pointed the weapons at two of the pirates. The two approached him slowly. Their legs trembled and their heads hung low. He motioned for the men to move to the edge of the water, and they did as they were told. One of them had a piece of bright cloth tied around his forehead. Andrew realized with a start that it was Hairy Arm!

Next, the tall man stuck the pistols out in front of him, cocking them to fire. Was he going to shoot Hairy Arm and the other pirate in cold blood? The tall man lifted one foot and pivoted his body around in a half circle. Now his guns were aimed at the tree where Andrew hid!

Andrew looked around wildly. Had the tall pirate spotted his hiding place? Andrew considered jumping off the branch and mak-

ing a run for it. He wondered if gunfire could reach him from the water's edge? Perhaps he should surrender and throw himself at the tall man's mercy.

The tall man walked stiffly up the beach, holding his arms straight out, his guns aimed at Andrew's chest! Andrew realized the man's eyes were shut. What was going on?

Suddenly, the tall man whirled around to face the sea. Shots rang out! One of the pirates fell backward, screaming. It was Hairy Arm! Andrew watched, openmouthed, as the landscape jumped to life. Men were running, shouting. Someone lifted Hairy Arm's head out of the water. A dark-skinned pirate moved to the side of the tall man who had shot Hairy Arm. The dark pirate gently took the arm of the bearded man. He asked, "Why'd ye do that, Captain?"

Andrew gasped. The tall man, the smoking volcano—he was the captain! The famous Blackbeard had shot at his own crew!

Blackbeard turned to the dark pirate at his side. Andrew could see Blackbeard's face clearly now. Horrified, Andrew saw that a smile had spread across the man's features. Calmly, the pirate captain adjusted a bit of red fabric in his beard, then spoke these words: "If I do not kill one of ye now and then, ye'll forget who I am!" With that, Captain Blackbeard began to laugh, long and hard. It was the laugh of a lunatic.

Andrew's notion of becoming a pirate evaporated like dew. He had but one thought left in his head: escape from Blackbeard Island!

Andrew jumped from the tree and tore through the forest. He never looked back. His mind kept returning to Blackbeard's wicked smile and his horrid laughter. Andrew Henson ran faster than he had ever run before.

At last he reached the end of the forest. He gaped. Where was the marsh he had crossed only twelve hours earlier? Before him was a wide river. Had he gotten lost?

Afraid to retrace his path, Andrew plunged into the water. He found it was only waist high. He was walking on grasses, not sand. Had the marsh flooded? It was difficult to walk through the brackish water. It swirled around him, pulling him and then pushing him back. But he could see the land on the far side of the creek. He prayed he was crossing over to Sapelo.

The water became deeper. Andrew began to swim. His progress was slow, and he was beginning to tire. He seemed to be fighting the current, rather than moving forward. But the memory of that insane laughter drove him on. He had to get away from Blackbeard Island!

Andrew's eyes smarted from the sun and the salt. Was his imagination playing tricks, or was that a boat coming toward him? He stopped stroking and tread water, straining to see. Yes! It was a boat! He squinted. It was much smaller than the pirate ship.

Andrew bobbed up and down, waving his arms over his head. "Here I am!" he shouted. "Here! Over here!"

As the vessel pulled nearer, Andrew recognized his stepfather's boat. Andrew had never been so glad to see any reminder of his stepfather. He nearly wept at the thought of the peaceful farm. He heard James, his stepfather's overseer, call out, "I'm throwing out a line! Grab the rope and pull yourself in."

"Pirates!" Andrew gasped as he fell into the boat. "The pirates tied me up." James offered Andrew water to drink. Greedily, the boy chugged great mouthfuls. "We've got to hurry! Blackbeard, he shot the pirate with the hairy arms. I saw it with my own eyes. We've got to get out of here. Away from Blackbeard Island!"

James smiled, rowing calmly. "You must have caught the fever, Andrew. It's a good thing I came looking for you. You might have drowned. It's a foolish thing to go off by yourself. What will your stepfather say?"

"You don't understand. I saw the pirate Blackbeard! Really, I did! The man's a murderer. Shot at his own crew. Hairy Arm fell in the ocean. Probably dead. And smoke was coming out of the captain's beard!"

The man began to laugh. "Andrew Henson, who's been filling your head with pirate tales? You did not see any pirate Blackbeard. But you nearly got yourself stranded over on Blackbeard Island. Didn't you know this creek would fill up when the tide came in?"

"I promise I saw pirates. They tied me up. They were going to make me ship's boy. They gave me this." Andrew fumbled with the hem of his shirt. He pulled out the coin.

James took the coin. He turned it over in the palm of his hand, examining it. "This is a beauty, son. Doubloon, I think. 'Twas a stroke of luck to find such booty in the sand. I wonder what poor wreck of a vessel left that coin to the waves? The sea washes up all sorts of mysteries."

"I didn't find it in the sand," Andrew said. "Hairy Arm gave it to me. So I wouldn't holler out. You see..."

"It's no good, Andrew," said James patiently. "If your stepfather flogs you for running off, you'd best take it like a man. It's no good making up wild tales about pirates and such."

"But I'm not making it up!" Andrew protested.

The fellow's patience had run out. "Look, son. I'm fond of reading about pirates myself. I've read the stories about the famous pirate Captain Blackbeard. It's common knowledge that he sometimes put smoking candles in his beard to scare people.

"Fact is, you couldn't have seen Captain Blackbeard. Because Blackbeard is dead! Been dead for fifty years."

All color drained from Andrew's face. "Blackbeard is dead?" Was James playing tricks on him? Andrew had seen Blackbeard with his own eyes. Heard the horrible laughter. Hadn't he?

"Yes, Andrew. Blackbeard is dead. He was killed off the coast of North Carolina. One of the officers in His Majesty's Navy hunted him down. Lieutenant Robert Maynard was the officer's name. It's a famous story. Maynard even cut off the villain's head. Hung it on the mast of his ship for all to see. The battle was in November of 1718, if my memory serves me. And this is 1768. So, Blackbeard was killed exactly fifty years ago. Fifty years ago, to the month."

Andrew stared at the golden coin in his hand. He could see the dents his teeth had made in the metal. He squinted. No, it was not his imagination. He was sure he could see another set of teeth marks on the coin!

PIRATES AND THE BARRIER ISLANDS

Blackbeard Island sits like a cap at the northeastern tip of Sapelo Island. It is now a National Wildlife Refuge. It has been called Blackbeard Island since the 1760s, but nobody knows why it was named after the famous pirate captain. There persists a popular belief that pirates landed on the island and perhaps buried treasure there. Actually, no evidence of pirate activity has ever been found on Blackbeard Island or anywhere else along Georgia's coast!

Some people call the islands along Georgia's Atlantic coast the Golden Isles because legends tell of buried pirate gold. Others point to the warm golden sunshine as the source of the name. Throughout the centuries, these islands have been home to Native Americans, Spanish soldiers and missionaries, French sailors, and English settlers. The main islands include Cumberland, Jekyll, Sea Island, St. Simons, Blackbeard, Sapelo, St. Catherines, and Ossabaw.

ABOUT THE AUTHORS

Gail Karwoski and Lori Hammer met as teaching colleagues at their Oconee County school. The scarcity of Georgia storybooks suitable for their middle school readers inspired them to create *The Tree that Owns Itself.*

Loretta Johnson Hammer teaches fourth grade in Watkinsville, Georgia, where she has lived for almost twenty years. After graduating from Washburn University with a B.A., she received her M.Ed. and Ed.S. from the University of Georgia. Her play *Strong Man from Georgia* is a participant in *GEORGIA: STATE OF THE ARTS,* the cultural celebration sponsored by the Georgia Council for the Arts and the Atlanta Committee for the Olympic Games Cultural Olympiad.

Gail Langer Karwoski teaches intermediate-grade students in Watkinsville, Georgia. She received her B.A. from the University of Massachusetts and her M.A. from the University of Minnesota, later earning her elementary and gifted teaching certificates at the University of Georgia. The story "King of the Swamp" was supported in part by the Georgia Council for the Arts through appropriations from the Georgia General Assembly.